BLOODSTOCK

AND

BOURBON

CURIOUS TALES FROM KENTUCKY

CRAIG CAUDILL

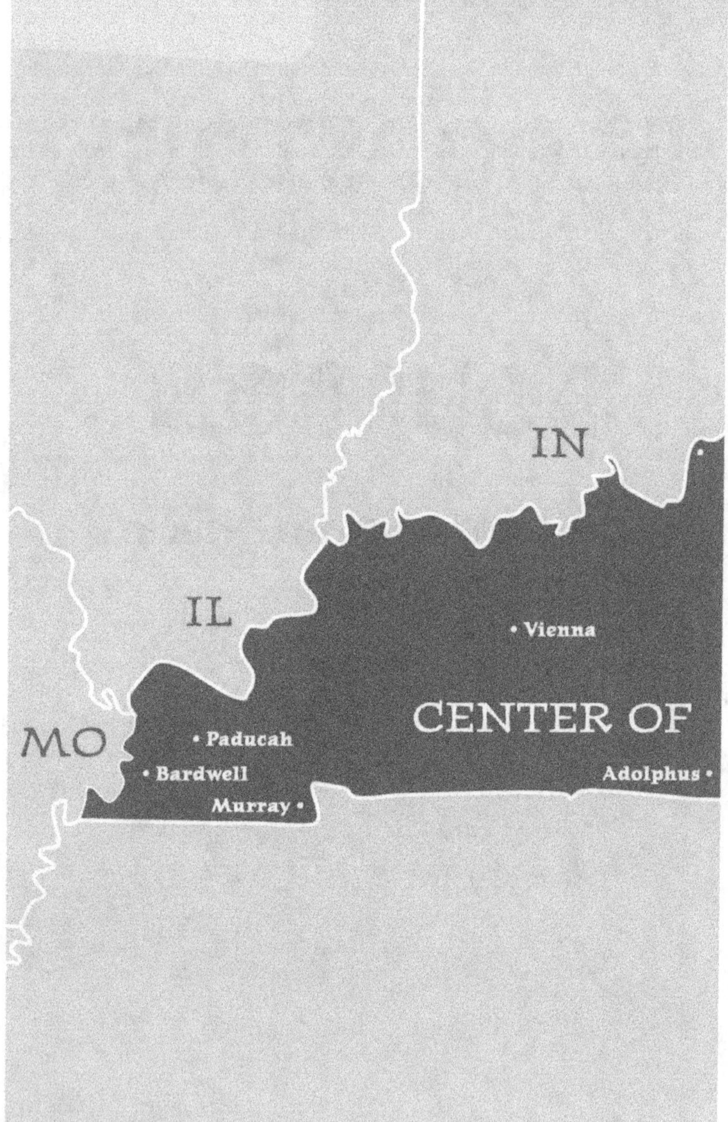

IN
IL
MO
Vienna
CENTER OF
Paducah
Bardwell
Murray
Adolphus

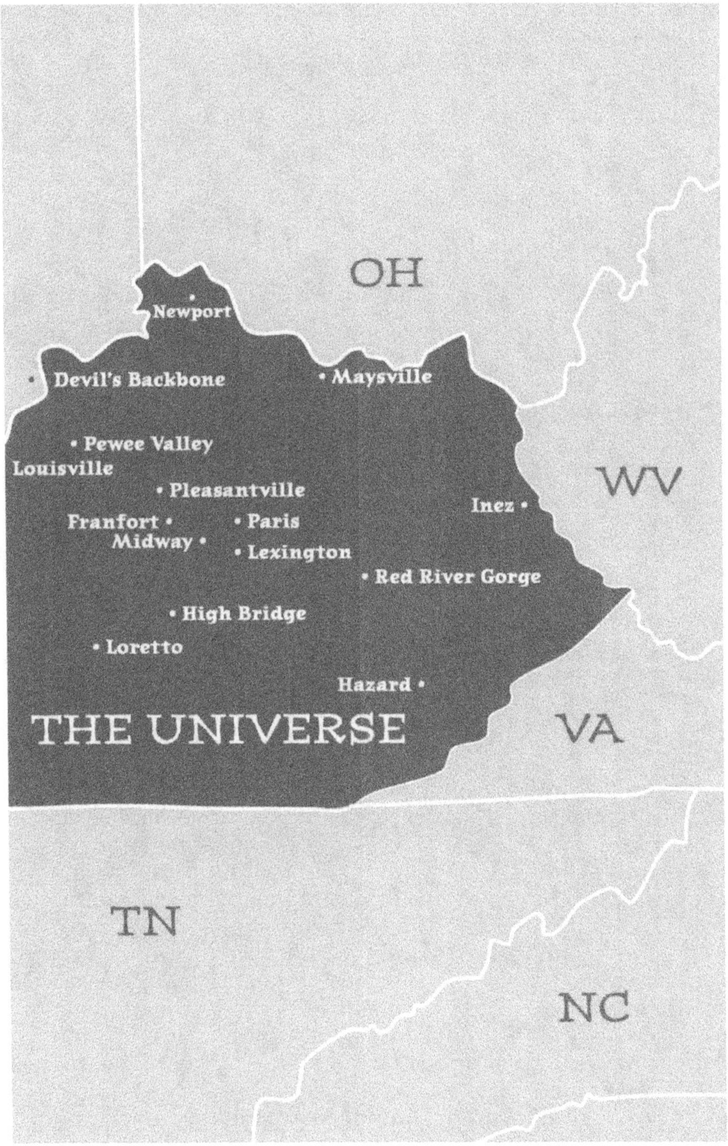

OH
WV
VA
TN
NC
Newport
Devil's Backbone
Maysville
Pewee Valley
Louisville
Pleasantville
Inez
Franfort
Paris
Midway
Lexington
Red River Gorge
High Bridge
Loretto
Hazard
THE UNIVERSE

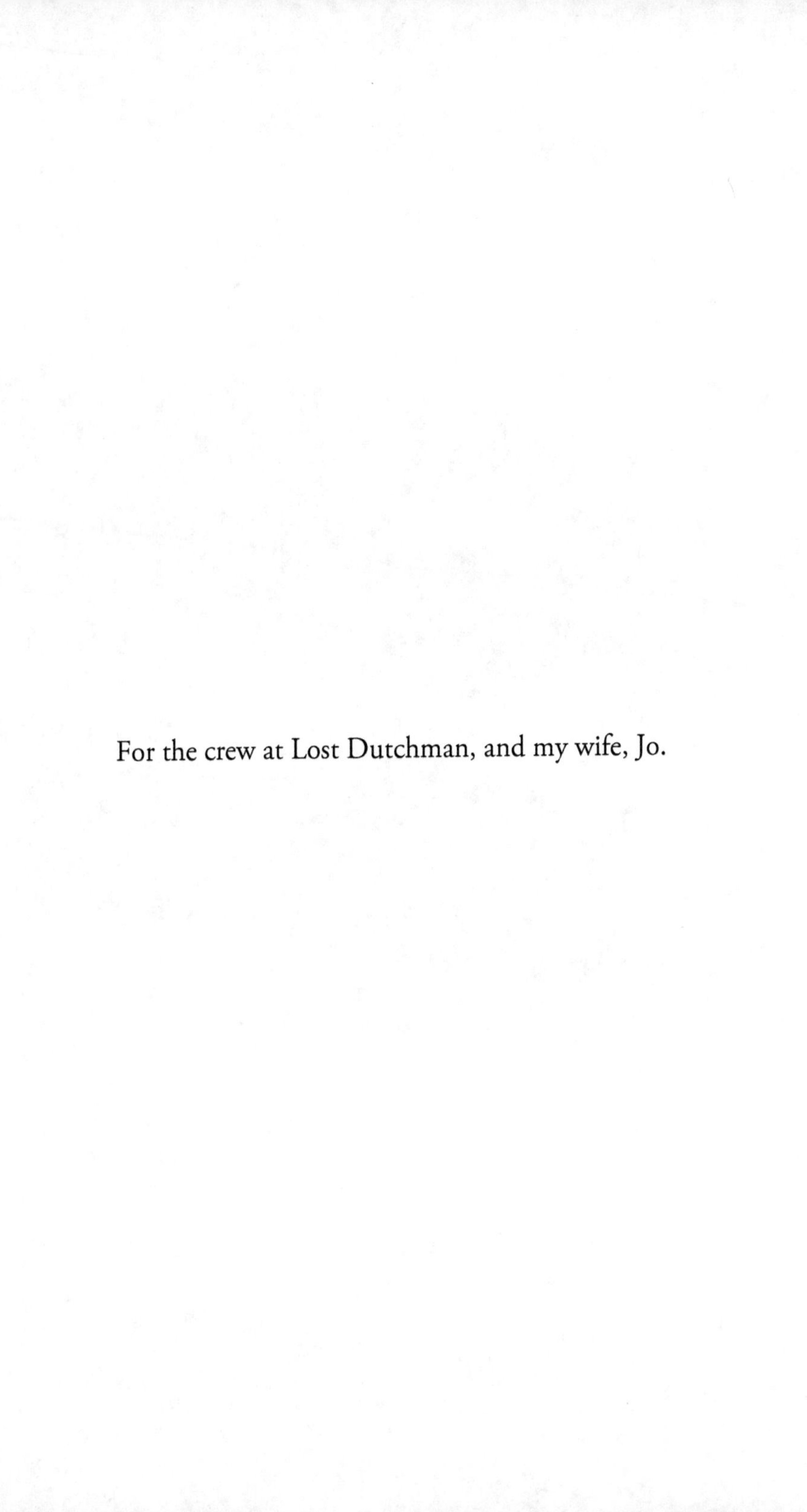
For the crew at Lost Dutchman, and my wife, Jo.

Contents

Dante's Hail Fire

TWENTY YEARS AGO

Penelope McDermott was a young, boyish Irish girl with a pixie blond ponytail, and could shoot the eye out of a sparrow at fifty yards. "Pull!" she yelled in the direction of the tin-clad bunker where Dante Regan had crouched to operate the clay pigeon thrower. He released the arm, heard the boom of the gun, and watched the defenseless target explode into shards and powder.

"Seven left!" Dante hollered out. A pounding headache came on him instantly from the pulsing report of the rifle.

"Send them out as fast as you can, like hail fire," she goaded. The orange bits of clay sparkled as they fell out of the sky in bursts. When all the shrapnel had landed harmlessly in the field, she propped the smoking skeet gun up against the horse barn with a sense of finality and fleetingly basked in the glory of a moot victory over a box of clay pigeons.

Dante Regan, who loved Penelope keenly, was a ham-handed mesomorph with russet hair and zaffre-blue eyes. He spryly popped up out of the bunker and said, "Good shooting." Dante felt like the pigeon himself sometimes when she got hyper-competitive like this. The two of them had been an item going on three years now since graduating the same year from St. Mary's Secondary School in Nenagh, County Tipperary. He knew how she was, and her him, but for some inexplicable reason, she kept him around as her boy toy, the penniless beau.

"Thanks. Let's get back at it," she ordered. Penelope worked in the office at Golden Oak Stud. Dante trained the half dozen or so racehorses on the farm. The 100-acre spread, owned by Cameron Fitzgerald, was located in the sweetest part of the Golden Vale region of Ireland. Other thoroughbred operations in the area considered Golden Oak somewhat of a joke, yet Fitzgerald was bound and determined to produce a winning racehorse, or go broke trying.

Dante said, "Hey, Penny, I've got some news. I'm flying to Kentucky next week. My cousin called and asked me to visit him at Churchill Downs. He's a trainer there. I'm pretty excited to see how they do things."

"Good for you. How long you gonna be gone?" she asked.

"Two weeks."

"Have a nice time," she commented with only a hint of jealousy.

Lorcan Power, Dante's cousin, had a round face, florid complexion, brown eyes, and shock of black hair. He stood outside the windy Louisville airport terminal at midday on Friday and barked, "How was your flight?" The deep-throated roar of planes taking off kept the conversation rudimentary.

"Long."

Lorcan ignored that and said, "Have you ever played Powerball?"

"I don't know what that is," Dante replied as they climbed into Lorcan's car.

"Well, you're about to find out." He wheeled into the first gas station they saw and parked off to the side of the convenience store. "For two dollars, you select five numbers between one and sixty-nine and then a Powerball number from one to twenty-six. If you match some or all of them, you win money. I play it all the time." Dante silently took a pencil out of his pocket and wrote down random numbers on the back of his plane-ticket jacket. Lorcan urged, "Come on, I'll show you how to buy a ticket."

"When do they draw the numbers?"

"Saturday night."

The cousins spent the rest of the day relaxing and talking about training horses. Lorcan's apartment had the distinct effluvium of horse dung. The beds and kitchen were clean enough, and the big-screen TV was first rate. They went out and picked up some Old Forester sippin' bourbon and corned beef sandwiches to munch on while watching the St. Louis Cardinals baseball game the rest of Friday evening.

Churchill Downs at seven a.m. on a Saturday morning in June reminded one of Grand Central Station. Dozens of people stood at the rail, swiveling their heads at each animal that sped by. The labored breathing of several horses at once sounded like snoring drunks in a hunting lodge bunkhouse. Lorcan took a few rambunctious thoroughbreds from the barns over to the track for workouts. With a curled brow, Dante observed everything that went on and experienced a bit of a revelation—training racehorses was big business, really hard work, and very scientific. He felt silly and amateurish at that moment. He knew he would have to up his game significantly to make a good living at it.

Lorcan and Dante were dead tired when they entered Lorcan's air-conditioned apartment later that evening. Both men kicked off their boots that had worn out their welcome before gulping down several glasses of ice water from the refrigerator. They turned on the local TV channel that featured the Powerball drawing and flopped on the couch from exhaustion. Lorcan got his pencil ready to jot down the winning numbers. He grumbled and sighed with each draw. "Mine's a bust," he said. "Where's yours?"

Dante said, "I don't know." He stood up and dug in his pants pocket until he found the ticket. "Read the numbers off to me." He hesitated for a moment, looked up, and said serenely, "They all match."

A six-number winning Powerball ticket paid forty million dollars over thirty payments unless a smaller, lump-sum amount was preferred. The residual came to a little over sixteen million dollars after the one-time tax hit. Dante dialed up Penny at the end of two weeks to tell her something had come up, and that he would have to extend his stay in Kentucky. She sounded only mildly disappointed. He didn't want anyone other than Lorcan to know he'd won the Powerball.

It took a few weeks for the money to come through, and when it did, Dante purchased bullion with 98 percent of it. He found a reputable place where the gold could be safely stored in secrecy. Twenty percent of the stash was put in Lorcan Power's name. Dante also gave Lorcan some cash as a thank-you for introducing him to the Powerball game.

It had been seven weeks since Dante left Ireland and four days since he'd last talked to Penny. When she came on the phone, he said, "I should be home in about a week." No immediate response came. "Penny?"

"Dante, I'm going to marry Cameron Fitzgerald."

"What? How long has this been going on?" He felt his stomach tighten into a knot.

"Just happened recently. When you get back, he wants you to get your things and clear out. I'm sorry, Dante."

"Yeah, I bet you are," he replied caustically, and cut the line.

TEN YEARS AGO

Gold bullion hadn't been a particularly good investment for the cousins until two years ago when it began skyrocketing in value. The original sixteen million dollars had become a cool sixty-four million dollars. That made Dante and Lorcan mighty happy, so they wisely sold out for cash.

Dante Regan, who now went by the name Jacopo Infanti, learned to speak perfect Italian, and for years had been discreetly training horses for the most successful barns on the Italian racing circuit. With a huge pile of cash at his disposal, he decided to tell Lorcan about the dream he'd had since being thrown off Golden Oak Stud ten years ago. Lorcan grinned and declared that he knew the perfect place to make that dream come true.

Allen County, on the Kentucky side of the Tennessee border, at the longitudinal midpoint of the state, had the same topography as Golden Vale in Ireland. The town of Adolphus near the state line, population 300, featured a grocery store, gas station, bank, and not much else. West of town, Conch Hollow Road saw little or no traffic as it meandered westward through jaw-dropping countryside. Barrio Hill Road ran straight along the border, forty feet on the Tennessee side of the line. The cousins bought a parcel that was eleven square acres wide and thirty-eight tall. Lorcan deeded the lower half in his name, and Dante registered the upper half under his Italian name, Jacopo Infanti.

Gravel roads were put in up to Conch Hollow and down to Barrio Hill as north and south exits to the properties. Tall rows of arborvitae were planted on both sides of the gravel entrances to obfuscate what was behind the trees, which was a twelve-foot high, black-metal electrified fence that ran the perimeter of the acreage. A stone wall was built between the two farms that had massive, arched, wrought-iron gates that were left open during the daytime.

Lorcan opted to build a one-mile dirt-and-turf training track with a lake in the middle of it in the northcentral part of his property. Above the final turn of the track, he put in a yellow-and-brown, twelve-stall barn with a guest apartment on each end. Pastureland marked by white fencing ran along the property line accessible by walkways to the barn. He built a southern-style, antebellum brick house for himself a little further north. He only had $200,000 left to his name after fitting the barn out and paying for elaborate landscaping. His first serious customer would be Dante Regan, who had warned him to never use that name again, the man who had made it all possible.

Jacopo's budget was considerably larger than Lorcan's, and so was the scope of his construction project. As a young boy, Dante had visited Dalhousie Castle in Scotland. He intended to build a duplicate of it fifty yards north of the stone wall that divided the cousin's properties.

Indigenous limestone blocks were used to construct the magnificent structure that took nearly three years to build. From the front, the right side was a rectangular, three-story affair with small turrets at the corners and crenelated battlements around the perimeter of the parapets. The chimneys were tall, as was the arched entrance biased to the left side. The large round tower further to the left imposed dramatically on the English-style, gravel parking lot that ran the entire width of the castle. Two more stories of penthouse, better seen from the back, overlooked the rear of Lorcan's house, the barn, and training track. Dante installed security and surveillance cameras virtually everywhere, including in all twelve stalls of the barn.

Jacopo Infanti became a regular at the Keeneland sales. He usually bought two horses a year for the Italian barns he represented, would board them elsewhere until they were two years old, and then bring them out to Lorcan's barn to begin training them. When they were ready to race, he'd ship them to Italy. Infanti worked strictly on commission, which meant he took a cut of a horse's lifetime winnings.

Lorcan Power approached the business differently. He boarded and trained horses for Irish farms that wanted to race colts and fillies in America. More times than not, the form of an Irish thoroughbred would be darkened before being sent over in the hopes of springing an upset in a stakes race and cashing a big pari-mutuel ticket. Lorcan's job simply consisted of preparing the horses to fire.

ONE YEAR AGO

Sean Fitzgerald, Penelope's eighteen-year-old son, came into the main house from the barn seething from a bad attitude. "Why am I busting my ass around here for nothing?" He slammed his work gloves down on the dining room table and peered loathsomely at his mother.

"Because your father can't afford to pay the help. If you don't like it, ship out, make it on your own." She was even bitterer about the situation than her boy, but would never be the first to admit defeat. The other farms in Golden Vale made sure that Cameron Fitzgerald never got any good horses to train and race. They were getting close to squeezing him out and buying his prime farmland, and if they pulled it off, she had already resolved to leave him.

Sean and Penelope heard Cameron Fitzgerald's truck and trailer arc around in front of the house before coming to a stop. Cameron jumped out and burst through the door of the house like a fireman searching for a conflagration. Short of breath, he shouted, "You're not going to believe it. That horse I claimed last month is one spectacular animal. He'd only run right-handed until today. I put him in a left-handed race this afternoon, and he damn near broke the track record."

Sean asked, "What's his name?"

"Dieselmore. Come outside and take a look at him." He beckoned them with both of his hands. The horse stuck his bristly nose through the window of the trailer and snorted two funnels of air out of his nostrils in an affectionate hello.

Penelope concluded, "We'll have to take him to America then."

ONE WEEK AGO

Jacopo left for Italy a few weeks after the Kentucky Derby to deliver two racehorses and visit his colorful Italian clients. He got an unexpected call from Lorcan one afternoon when he was explaining the training regimen for the new horses to the barn staff. "What's up?" he asked.

"Dante, a guy and his family are rolling in here today with a horse that they claim is unbeatable. They're looking for a match race and are willing to bet a lot of money that the horse can beat all comers."

"Lorcan, I've asked you not to call me Dante. It's Jacopo."

"Right, sorry. All you have here is Hail Fire, who is a work in progress. What should I do?"

"Who are these people?"

"Cameron and Penelope Fitzgerald and their son, Sean."

"What? How did they find you?"

"I advertise in Ireland. They found me that way, I guess. Do you know them?"

"Here, look. Put them up in the castle, and for heaven's sake, don't utter the name Dante Regan to them or anyone else. Got that?"

"Yep. Any ideas on how we can beat them?" Lorcan asked.

"I'll think on it."

Cameron Fitzgerald remained a proud man even if he was stony broke. His wife didn't give a fig about pride—she wanted to be rich enough to thumb the eye of the Golden Vale horsy set. She knew that Dieselmore was her last chance at victory and serious money. Cameron and Sean unloaded the colt carefully and escorted him to his assigned stall in the barn. Lorcan said, "You folks can drive right through there. My neighbor, Jacopo Infanti, told me you are welcome to stay in his castle while you're here with us. He said he'd be home in a few days. I'm sure you'll be well taken care of."

Penelope whistled and said, "Will you look at that place. How'd he make the money to build such a thing?"

"He trains racehorses in Italy. Works on commission. I guess it's been a good decision."

Jacopo called Lorcan from Italy later in the week to ask, "Did Fitzgerald say how much he wanted to bet on a match race?"

"Yes. He's willing to bet two hundred and fifty thousand. He offered his Irish farm as collateral."

"Tell him we'll take the bet. I'll send a document to you for him to sign."

"Who are you going to race against his horse?"

"Hail Fire."

"Bad idea," Lorcan said before telling Fitzgerald that Hail Fire would race Dieselmore straight up, one mile, left handed, in three days. Jacopo called a solicitor in Ireland and asked him to check for liens on the Fitzgerald farm. The property had a value of two million US dollars and bank liens of 1.8 million dollars, as it turned out.

YESTERDAY

Dante Regan drove one of his horse trailers from the Nashville airport to Lorcan's barn late on a dusty afternoon two days later and surreptitiously unloaded a monster of a horse that was muscled and cut like Man o'War on steroids. The name that glistened on the brass bridle plate read Grandine Fuoco.

TODAY

Dieselmore emerged from the barn area, looking relaxed and confident. Right behind him came Grandine Fuoco. Sean Fitzgerald piped up, "Hey, that's not the horse that's been training around here the last few days. That thing is a giant." He pointed at the thoroughbred, and his mouth dropped open in awe.

"The horse's name is *Grandine Fuoco.* That's Italian for hail fire," Lorcan said. The bug riders were hoisted up on the two colts, and they galloped with purpose down the backstretch. When the contestants swung back around on the final turn and into the homestretch, the starting gate loomed a short distance ahead of them.

Jacopo Infanti sat in the surveillance room at the castle, intending to watch the match race from there. Dozens of cameras were broadcasting every bit of activity happening on the properties. He saw the starting gate fly open without a sound, and it was clear that Grandine Fuoco was going to make Dieselmore lead, even if they had to walk. Both colts drifted wide in the homestretch. Dieselmore led by two lengths. A furlong later, Grandine Fuoco crossed the finish line five lengths in front.

Cameron and Sean stood in the infield, dejected, heads down. Sean began shuffling erratically in the direction opposite the barn. Cameron grabbed the reins of Dieselmore when the rider jumped off, and started leading the beaten horse back up the homestretch toward the barn.

Jacopo got distracted by some movement in the camera located on the penthouse parapet. On the screen, Penelope held a scoped rifle over the wall, aimed at the final turn of the training track. She pulled the trigger, and in another camera shot, half of Cameron Fitzgerald's throat disappeared, and he crumpled to the ground. Penelope ducked, disassembled the rifle in fifteen seconds, loaded it into a wooden case, and scurried to the door that led off the roof. Jacopo hopped up and ran through the castle at full speed until he reached the hall where she would emerge. When she did, he stated with malice aforethought, "The bastard deserved it for stealing my girlfriend."

Penelope halted with a start and appeared to be in shock. "What did you say?"

"Penny, honey, I'm Dante Regan. Remember me?" Her knees almost buckled, and a case of the vapors overtook her.

"Oh, no," she cried out as she slid down the wall onto the floor.

"I'm sure Lorcan is calling the police right now. I suggest that you steal the car that I use to go back and forth to the Nashville airport. The keys are in it." Penny looked up at him in disbelief. "You can never go back to Ireland. If you're able to escape from here and get to Italy, look me up there. I'll sign the deed to Golden Oak over to your son and pay off the liens on it."

Penelope said nothing and struggled to get to her feet.

"Maybe someday you'll be able to return here as Donna Infanti."

As she pulled away in the car going north, the police sirens could be heard closing in from the south.

Diamond Off a Queen's Ring

At twilight, the wind surged and spritzes of drizzle peppered the Highland Festival Grounds at the Kentucky Expo Center in Louisville. The jubilant Bourbon & Beyond crowd barely noticed the inclement weather as eager fans pushed forward inexorably to catch a closer glimpse of the band. The Ludds, stationed in an arc around the stage, kept the beat on "The Thrill is Gone" as zany front man, Vandal Harm, masterfully strummed a low-slung '59 Stratocaster while belting out the words of the blues standard in his idiosyncratic, smoky voice.

Vandal Harm and the Ludds had hit the big time. Harm became a virtuoso by way of a gimmick once employed by Jimi Hendrix and Stevie Ray Vaughn. He used open E-flat tuning on one guitar, a half-step down, reducing the tension on the strings, making it easier to bend the notes. His group was known as a great blues cover band until the song "Diamond Off a Queen's Ring" came out. The truly original tune, and Harm's quirkiness, fueled the breakthrough.

Darkness set in at the venue, and the wispy rain lightened considerably. Vandal stepped to the microphone and said, "Before we do our last song, I want to tell you a story. My girlfriend and I broke up five years ago, and we agreed to meet here at this festival five years later. Who knew I'd be playing." He paused for effect. "If it was meant to be, we'd know it when we met again.

Are you here Consuela?" He hooded his eyes against the stage lights and peered out into the crowd.

Consuela Dimick yelled out, "I'm here!" She waved her hand over her head and bounced up and down, some 100 feet out from the stage. Vandal could see well enough to tell that she was even more beautiful than he remembered.

"I'll see you after the show!" The throng of people roared in anticipation, and the Ludds broke into "Diamond Off a Queen's Ring,"which brought down the house.

FIVE YEARS AGO

Jerome Dimick came to Kentucky as a young lawyer twenty years earlier and bought the 1860 Orman Barnett House in the Victorian section of Old Louisville. The gable-fronted, redbrick structure had bracketed eaves, paneled frieze below the cornice, and recessed diamond-paned windows. He and his wife Mary raised their daughter Consuela in local society and sent her to the best private schools. They were very disappointed when Consuela announced that she intended to enroll at Murray State University that fall instead of Vanderbilt, Transylvania, or Butler.

Dimick's law partner, Garvis Pelletier, owned the 1884 Arnold Pryor House next door, done in the Queen Anne style that featured a projecting bay, curved corners, lathed posts, and art glass. The Pelletier's only son, Bodie, became best friends with Consuela. Both families were hoping that a romance would strike up between them, leading to marriage and lots of children. As Bodie and Consuela were preparing to go off to college, Garvis and Myrna Pelletier had no intention of letting their son matriculate at Murray State alongside Consuela and the hoi polloi. Besides, Bodie, a prodigy of sorts, wanted to go to a fine music school where he could become a better songwriter and musician.

Consuela arrived on the campus of Murray State in the harsh sunlight that radiated down on the Wednesday morning after Labor Day. She began to have misgivings about her college choice when intense loneliness beset her during a rainstorm forty-eight hours later. She knew no one, and there weren't any gentry in plain sight that she could rub elbows with. To be sure, Consuela felt completely out of place. Her decision to attend Murray State had been driven solely by her desire to break free from her parents and see how the other half lives. She decided to go hear a group that had been touted as the best blues band around, to get her mind off her predicament. That's when she first met Vandal Harm.

Harm hailed from a secluded, Spartan farmhouse he owned near Mayfield, Kentucky, not more than fifty miles from campus. He was a twenty-two-year-old senior, having spent the first three years of his college experience learning how to read, write, and play music the right way. He had taught himself guitar at age eleven, but yearned to understand proper technique and the language of music. He played in as many gigs as he could get to pay his tuition and living expenses. Vandal knew how to handle money. It was the oddball streak that made him ignominious in the eyes of the enlightened. That didn't stop a cult of the unenlightened from swelling around him.

Consuela and Vandal saw each other nearly every day for the next three weeks. The relationship quickly moved past friendship, and Consuela began to get nervous. "Van, I don't think we can do this," she said. "I hate it here. I'm going to withdraw from my classes and go back home." Her facial expression became contorted, and the corners of her eyes crinkled up.

"Connie, I'm not one to tell other people what to do. I say live and let live. I don't have to like it, though. You're special, and I'll be brokenhearted when you're gone."

She looked directly at him and offered a quivery smile. "You need to finish your degree and make it in the music business. I need to regroup and figure out what I'm doing with my life." She turned away and gazed out the window at the students streaming along wearing backpacks. A guy that looked like Bodie Pelletier from the back moved off behind the fountain in the middle of campus. He reminded her of what she missed. "How about this. Let's meet up again in five years at the Bourbon Festival in Louisville. That will give us time."

"I'm already counting the days," he replied as he stood up. "You'll let me see you off when you leave, won't you?"

"Yes," she added sotto voce.

THREE YEARS AGO

Vandal went to Nashville after graduation to find a group of studio musicians that he could hire to make a record. He rebuilt the band to include a rhythm guitar, organ, bass, and drums. His reputation as a player attracted some of the finest studio musicians in the city. They liked how he treated people, and that he always paid in cash. He told them before leaving town, "I'll let you know when I've got a dozen songs ready. I'm pretty open to suggestions except when it comes to playing the guitar. Oh, by the way, the name of our band is the Ludds."

The drummer piped up, "Say what?"

"Haven't you heard Robert Calvert's song?" Vandal suddenly became wild-eyed.

"Well, no, I haven't," the drummer responded.

"They said Ned Ludd was an idiot boy. That all he could do was wreck and destroy. He turned to his workmates and said, 'Death to machines. They tread on our future, and they stamp out our dreams.'"

The organ player asked him, "Are you a Luddite?"

"Somewhat, and much more than that," he chirped on the way out the door.

Meanwhile, Bodie Pelletier was attending Indiana University and had gained admission to the School of Music based on a demo tape he submitted of a song where he played and overdubbed all of the instruments. Consuela got into Vanderbilt and had already completed three semesters toward a sociology degree. Bodie and Consuela ran around together during summer break, rekindling the hope among their parents of an amorous affair. He trotted out a copy of the demo tape for her when she asked him how he was able to get into music school.

TWO YEARS AGO

The organist stopped in the middle and said, "Hold it. Why don't I take my part down an octave and make it a little choppier? Like this." He played his version several times to elicit comments from the others.

"Sounds great," Harm affirmed. "If we're going to do that, let's slow it down and let the drums hang slightly behind the beat." The band picked up where it left off, changing the feel of the rhythm on the fly. "Okay, we'll rehearse three more times, and get it on tape."

It took the Ludds four weeks to knock out a dozen songs. About half of them were new music that Vandal had written. The rest were obscure Texas shuffles, rumbas, and reggaes. He was sure of one thing: nothing there would catch the eye of a critic. Like all songwriters, he lived on the dream of writing that one masterpiece that would shoot to the top and take the band with it.

The album came out as a vinyl record with a cover that folded open. The front had been done in slick white with the large, faint-gray words *Liberating Freedom* across the top. Small, black script identified the name of the band at the bottom left. The only other thing on the cover was an embossed, quartering perspective of the maroon 1966 Pontiac GTO that Vandal drove.

The words inside the fold, not the music, continued to ramp up Harm's following.

CREED OF THE LUDDS (on the left inside cover)

Liberate yourself from the slavery of technology

> • *No television, email, social media, smartphone, or internet*

Liberate yourself from poisonous processed foods

> • *Eat wild-caught seafood, and natural, organically-grown foods*

Liberate yourself from the greedy money changer

> • *No banks, loans, credit cards, payments,—deal only in cash*

Liberate yourself from the oppression of backward nations

> • *Travel the US, buy American made, listen to American music*

WHAT WE DO (on the right inside cover)

THANK GOD

LOVE FAMILY

WORK HARD

EAT RIGHT

READ VORACIOUSLY

THINK CRITICALLY

BE CHARITABLE

BE FORGIVING

BE KIND

The back cover of the album listed the names of the twelve songs on the record.

Vandal Harm and the Ludds began playing a lot of live gigs around the Midwest and South. They built a following much like The Grateful Dead and Phish.

ONE YEAR AGO

Bodie Pelletier asked Consuela, "Where exactly is our relationship going?"

"Come now, we've known each other our whole lives," she said, trying to deflect him. He had been hopelessly drawn in by her pulchritude that increased with each passing day.

"Does that mean we're like brother and sister?" The tone of his voice switched to a baleful timbre.

"No. We should get through school first and find our places in life before any courtship." She had given Vandal Harm the same speech, only using different words.

"That's horse manure, if I may say so." Bodie thought about walking out and never speaking to her again. Consuela became angry with that remark and told him about her encounter years ago with Vandal at Murray State. He felt a knot in the pit of his stomach.

The second go-around, Vandal Harm had twelve original songs ready to record. There was one in the bunch that he had worked to death for three years. He thought it might just be a *Mona Lisa*.

Diamond Off a Queen's Ring

Went over to the man
To get my baby a spiff
Like a pea under the mattress
I felt it and wondered what if?

A diamond
Off a queen's ring
Lyin' in the parking lot
A diamond
On my baby
Can see her bein' so hot

He took a good look
Said it was plenty real
That big lump on her finger
Surely'd make boys' eyes peel

This diamond
Off a queen's ring
Found in the parking lot
My diamond
For my baby
Why not give it a shot?

Bought a flashy band
Told him to put it atop
Like a beacon bird perched
Only the question left to pop

That diamond
Off a queen's ring
Gone from the parking lot
Her diamond
She's my baby
Unless she finds out its hot

As the box flipped open
It was a pretty big shock
Like another gem she'd seen
It sparkled, was a mighty rock

The diamond
Off her Mom's ring
Lost in the parking lot
The next diamond
Where's my baby?
I'll leave in the parking lot

When the record hit the airwaves, the Ludds became famous instantly. The quality of the music, particularly Harm's guitar work, was off-the-charts good. The quirky guy from Western Kentucky and his band of studio musicians had delivered something tasty and unique.

AFTER THE SHOW

"My goodness, Consuela, you look wonderful," Harm said enthusiastically. His eyes twinkled with admiration.

"Thank you. Well, you've made it big. How does it feel?"

"Great. My guys are terrific musicians. So, what happened over the last five years?" Vandal tried to determine how she was different than when he last saw her. It was the fullness of her face, he surmised.

"I have a degree in sociology from Vanderbilt, but haven't taken a job yet," she replied.

"What about on the man front? Do you have one?"

A crease formed in her forehead. "Actually, one kind of has me."

"What do you mean?"

"The guy that has lived next door to me my whole life is threatening to ruin you if I don't marry him."

"What are you talking about?"

Consuela took the disc out of her pocket and lobbed it on the table. "He gave me this three years ago. It's a crude version of your hit song. He says he wrote it, and has a copyright on the words and music. He claims you stole it. He says he'll make a big stink and sue you for royalties if I don't marry him."

Harm's mind rolled through the possibilities. "I take it you don't want to marry the guy?"

"No. He lacks a little integrity, don't you think? And besides, I want to spend time with you," she said demurely.

"That's music to my ears. I can only see one way out of this, if things really happened the way I think they did," he said.

"You're not going to have him bumped off, are you?"

Vandal looked at her indignantly, and said, "That wasn't the first option that came to mind. Does he have a smartphone?"

"Sure."

"Your father's an attorney, right? You think he'd defend me if this goes to court?"

"If I told him to, he would, yes," she stated with certainty.

"Good. Here's the plan."

FIVE MONTHS LATER

Jerome Dimick sat next to Vandal Harm in court during the proceedings. Harm thought he could have quashed the lawsuit sooner, but felt that public vindication was important to his reputation. Across the aisle, Bodie Pelletier and his father, Garvis, had just finished presenting their case built on the idea that someone bootlegged to Vandal a copy of the song submitted to the music school. The judge announced, "The defense can proceed with its case."

"Your honor, Mister Harm wrote this music in longhand some years back, and it never left his farmhouse. We will show evidence that Bodie Pelletier broke into Harm's house and took pictures of the handwritten words and music with his smartphone. Mr. Pelletier then applied for and received a copyright on the song he had stolen."

Jerome Dimick explained how his daughter was taking photos with Bodie's phone recently when she noticed a picture of a handwritten song in the archives. She emailed it to herself out of curiosity. It turned out to be the song on his demo, so she assumed he'd taken the snapshot for some reason. After it became a Ludds hit, Bodie told Consuela that Harm had stolen it, and she got suspicious. When she looked again at the photo in her email of the handwritten song, the bottom of the page said, "Words and Music by Vandal Harm."

The judge asked Bodie to produce his phone. There was no such picture in the archives. The judge asked Vandal Harm if he still had the original of the song. He did not. Pelletier's copyright was upheld, and he was awarded royalties.

The next day, Consuela said to Vandal, "I can't believe that creep stole your music and got away with it."

"He did. It'll cost me about four hundred thousand initially, and no telling how much over the long haul. That'll teach me. Good thing is, I can afford to pay it. Bad thing is, my reputation has been damaged."

"Is there anything you can do about it?" Consuela asked.

"Maybe make my case to the public. I can take the picture you have of the song and prove that the handwriting is consistent with all of the other songs I've written."

"My father should have done that in the courtroom. I wonder if you can appeal the verdict?"

TWO MONTHS LATER

Garvis Pelletier and his son Bodie, and Jerome Dimick, and his daughter Consuela sat in the conference room of Dimick & Pelletier law offices and studied the check from Vandal Harm in the amount of $407,930. Garvis said to Jerome, "We pulled it off! Let's keep half of it in the firm and give a quarter each to Bodie and Consuela."

"Okay by me. Consuela, when are you going to break it off with Harm now that we've skinned him?" her father asked.

"There's no use waiting. I'll do it now."

She got in her car and started the long trip from Louisville to Western Kentucky. When Consuela was out of the city, she took in the rhododendrons, dogwoods, mountain laurel, and invasive Bradford pears that were in bloom everywhere. The brisk April air and rolling green hills lifted her mood a fair amount. A sense of satisfaction and calm came over her as she pulled into Harm's driveway two hours later.

Harm opened the weathered, craftsman-style door of his farmhouse, pulled her in close for a hug, and said, "I've missed you. How did everything go?" The smell of smoke from the woodburning fireplace had permeated his clothes.

"Perfectly." She pulled the tape recorder out of her pocket and played the morning conference-room conversation that she'd recorded for him. "You know, for a guy that hates technology, you should be thankful for it this time."

"I'll really like it when I get that royalty payment back and put it in that safe over there." He pointed at the massive, black box without looking in its direction.

"I love you, Van," is all she could think to say.

The Fall and Rise of the Third Porsche

Dieter Engel pulled his silver Carrera around the bend on Schulz Alley to an oil-stained parking spot he had been using since he first got his driver's license some fifty-plus years ago. Most anywhere in Maysville, Kentucky, a person could see the Ohio River unless it was really low, which happened to be this year because of the particularly dry fall and early winter weather. He had to crane his neck to check the color of the cold water flowing toward Louisville. The warmer than usual air on New Year's Eve hung like an invisible blanket over the little downtown area that would be coming to life after dark. His wife, Phoebe asked, "Are you feeling alright, Dieter?"

"Not really," he replied. "I've worked my tail off for fifty years, and now that I'm retiring, we've lost the business to a competitor that makes vegan burgers." He gritted his teeth, activated the emergency brake, pushed open the door, and threw his foot onto the pavement.

Phoebe got out and scolded him, "You should have been nicer to people along the way. Vicious men like you get what's coming to them. Frankly, you've been an embarrassment to me." She slammed the door and began walking in the direction of the restaurant and bar on Rosemary Clooney Street, where they were to meet up with the managers and spouses of the sausage business.

"Yeah," he said. Phoebe heard an odd scraping and thumping noise, and when she turned around to see what caused it, Dieter was face down on the ground with his head on the grass island and feet resting near the left-front tire of the Porsche. He was suffering from a catastrophic right-brain stroke from which he would never recover. While Phoebe waited for the ambulance to arrive, she looked up the hill at the garish sign on the brooding factory that read: Engel Sausage. She couldn't wait to get the hell out of that two-bit town she'd been stuck in for sixty years, so she could at least try to do something meaningful with what little life she had left.

Roy and Tonya Goins were less than a quarter of a mile away in the French Quarter section of Maysville, whooping it up, celebrating the purchase of the assets of Engel Sausage by their little company—Allied Foods. "Wonder what that ambulance is for?" Tonya remarked. She was trying to figure out if the expensive champagne they were drinking was worth the money. She and Roy had never availed themselves of extravagances like that before.

"Not sure. What do you think of that car we got in the deal?" Roy asked.

"Crazy-looking machine. Why'd you buy it anyway?"

"Because the bank said it was worth a couple of million dollars. We borrowed against it and used the money to buy the Engel business. The price for the equipment and car was one-and-a-half million, which is the amount the bank lent us on the car alone. We didn't have to put up a penny of our own money." Roy raised his glass and smiled like Gomer Pyle.

"Let's auction it off then, pay the bank back and use what's left over to grow sales." Tonya was more than a pretty face. She had good ideas and smart money sense.

"I like that," Roy said.

Stefan, Dieter's son, had been president of Engel Sausage for the last two years as a run-up to Dieter's retirement. He was much nicer than the old man, genuinely caring for other people. That proved to be part of the downfall of the company. All the enemies Dieter had made over the years among the grocers, competitors, and employees lined up to get their pound of flesh. Stefan's wife Niko cried every night over the nasty things that were said about the company and its business practices. Squaring up past injustices was not what actually killed it, though. The "meatless" movement did.

Tonya Goins came from a family of vegans. She learned from her mother how to make meat and animal-based cheese substitutes out of nuts. Roy Goins worked as a route salesman for Allied Foods, and when the owner wanted to retire, he sold the business to Roy for the value of the inventory. When Roy and Tonya married, she came into the business and began producing cultured-cashew products that she called "vegan cheeses." They became cult favorites among the health-food crowd. Next came sprouted seed-and-nut sausages and burgers that crushed the market share of Engel's Type 64 traditional meat sausages that had been the company's flagship product for over sixty years. Sales dropped precipitously at Engel, and the business was sold to pay off the bank debt.

A group of men from the auction company hired to sell the car owned by Allied Foods entered the climate-controlled garage where it was housed intending to do a complete inspection of the vehicle and prepare a slick with pertinent advertising data. The first thing the mechanic in the group did was look for the identification stamp 38/43 on the chassis and gearbox. He rolled out from under the car, sat up, and said, "This car is a replica. It ain't the real thing."

"What?" The auction-house salesman hopped around to confront the mechanic. "How can that be?"

"I don't know. The numbers aren't there."

"Well, how much is a replica worth?"

The mechanic pondered the question for a few seconds, and replied, "Maybe a hundred thousand max."

"Hell's bells, man. Our commission just went in the toilet. Worse yet, the lien on the thing from the bank is one-point-five mil." The salesman reached for his phone. "Roy, your car over here is a fake. Better get with that crooked Engel bunch and find out what they've done to you."

Dieter Engel, who Roy Goins did the purchase deal with, was dead, and his wife Phoebe had moved to Lexington. Roy went to the house of Stefan and Niko Engel the next morning in search of answers about the car. Niko opened the door to the frigid sunshine and smiled. She was wearing a purple caftan with side pockets and trapunto trim. "Hello, Roy. Won't you come in?"

"Thanks." She ushered him into the living room where her husband was seated. Stefan stood up and walked over near the fireplace to be courteous. "Hi there," Roy said cordially.

"Roy."

"The car your dad sold me has been switched out for a fake." Roy got right to the point.

"How do you know that?"

"Because the bank checked the identification numbers and photographed them *before the closing.* When I sent an auction house to check things out yesterday, the numbers weren't there. What do you know about the car?"

Stefan put his hands in his pockets and formed fists. "Everything," he said. "I've been around that hunk of junk my whole life." He remembered fondly the first time his Grandpa Horst took him for a ride in it when he was six years old.

"Have any ideas who might have had a replica built and been able to pull a swap?"

"It would have to be someone that knew the car inside out. To catch them, you might try to locate who built unique parts for a replica, and then find out who had them made."

"How do I do that?" Roy noticed the stunning pastel over the mantle depicting dancing women.

"Run ads that say *looking for parts maker for a Type 64 replica.*"

"You mean like your sausage?"

"Yes. My grandfather named our brand after the car."

"One thing's for sure, you and I need to find the real one, or we'll be in court with your family fighting over when the swap happened." Roy nodded at Niko and showed himself out.

Niko asked, "What's going on, Stefan?" He turned his back to her and propped his elbows on the mantle.

The Nazis were extremely proud of the Autobahn built in Germany during the 1930s. They intended to showcase the road system in a new race from Berlin to Rome, and needed to find the right person to build three aerodynamic roadsters to compete in the event. Enter one Ferdinand Porsche, the notorious car designer from Volkswagen and Mercedes. The German government authorized Volkswagen to supply him with the necessary mechanical parts, and the Porsche team had Reuter make lightweight aluminum bodies by hand. Sadly, the race was canceled after the start of World War II, but as it turned out, the cars got manufactured anyway by Ferdinand and his son Ferry. The sleek machines, known as Type 64, are recognized as the first ever to bear the Porsche name.

The three chassis were stamped: 38/41, 38/42, and 38/43. The silver-bodied 38/41, the first car to be built, was given to a Volkswagen board member who proceeded to wreck it. The black-painted 38/42, used for testing, stayed at the plant. The

38/43, also silver, was driven personally by Porsche family members. At the end of World War II, allied forces seized 38/42, cut the top off and used it for joy rides until the engine quit. Inexplicably, the body and engine from 38/43 were fitted onto the 38/41 chassis, and that conglomeration was sold to Otto Mathe, who raced it until 1953. The 38/41, with the 38/43 engine, had a perceived value of around $20,000,000. There were unsubstantiated reports in 1949 that the 38/43 chassis and remaining spare body and mechanical parts were sold by Porsche to Horst Engel, a businessman on his way to the United States, where he planned to open a new state-of-the-art sausage factory.

Horst Engel made his money during the war as a go-between for the Nazis and buyers of priceless artworks stolen from Jews. After the war, all sorts of people were tracking down those involved in stealing and selling art, and Horst began to get nervous. His relatives were sausage makers, so he decided to continue that tradition in America. He had not been part of the family business, but knew enough to make a go of it. In 1949, Horst worked in the Porsche factory as a machinist to lay low until he got his clearance to emigrate. That's when he learned about the parts of the third Type 64 that were still around the factory. He made an offer for them that Porsche couldn't refuse.

Horst picked Maysville, Kentucky as the place to set up shop because it was off the beaten path, yet close enough to Cincinnati and Pittsburgh where there were a whole bunch of Germans and sausage eaters. Being mechanically inclined, he built the best sausage-making machines in the world. He knew his recipe would be a hit because it was the most popular one in Germany. The secret was in the mixture of spices. He also used natural casings and eschewed fillers and other ways of cheapening the product. Horst called it "Engel's Type 64 Authentic German Sausage."

Horst and his wife Eva were rolling in money by 1955. Tragedy struck that year when she died giving birth to their son Dieter. Horst began restoring 38/43 to keep his mind off his sorrows.

Dieter was raised without a mother. By the time he entered the sausage business with his father, people knew that he would turn a "bunch of sweetness" into a "bag of filth." He went to every competitor and gave them an ultimatum: let Engel make their sausage or get pushed out of every major grocery store. Dieter had leverage with the grocery chains, and threw his weight around regularly. The employees were treated poorly too. They walked the other way when they saw him coming.

Horst retreated to the garage, where he tinkered endlessly with 38/43. He made regular trips to Germany to get parts, sometimes two or three of the same thing. As the parts piled up in the garage, he decided to build a replica that he could drive around in. The original car was too valuable to put miles on. He was seen whizzing all over Eastern Kentucky in the copy, always drawing a crowd of curious onlookers. When Horst died, his will conveyed everything to Dieter except for the authentic 38/43 and a painting he had brought over from Europe of five women dancing. They went to Stefan.

Phoebe Herzog moved to Maysville when she was very little. Her parents told her to marry for money. That's what she did when she hooked Dieter Engel, the richest man in town. He was a son-of-a-bitch to other people, but treated her fairly well. Otherwise, she would have left him. He also gave her a healthy and handsome son with a good disposition that she was thankful for. She felt no loss or pain when Dieter dropped dead. Maysville had been a bore to her for as long as she could remember. His death was her way out.

Stefan was dealt a bad hand when he stepped in to run Engel. Dieter had stripped all of the money out of it, and hadn't maintained the equipment or important relationships with vendors or customers. If the sausage wasn't absolutely delicious, the place would have folded years ago. The sales finally began to collapse when the "meatless" protein craze took hold. The debt at the bank piled up in a very short time. The only solution was to sell everything, including 38/43, that he hated anyway. Stefan and Niko ended up broke. Stefan's mother, Phoebe, had all the money.

Roy returned to the Engel house a month later. "Stefan, I've had no luck finding anything out about the car. I hope you've got a solution to this problem."

Stefan responded, "I do. Care for a bourbon?"

"No, thanks. What do you have in mind?" Roy moved over to the window to see how heavily the snow was falling. An inch of wet accumulation covered the grass. The gravel on the driveway remained visible.

"I think I know where the car is. We'll have to go get it together so one of us can drive it back. I suggest we wait until the roads dry off in a couple of days."

The snow had cleared by the third week in February when Roy and Stefan were running down the road in Stefan's twelve-year-old Porsche. The older machine still ran great, but rode like a proverbial hay wagon. "You care to tell me how you found the car?"

"It goes back to my grandfather. He restored the original and made a replica himself to ride around in."

"If you knew that, why'd you send me off chasing parts houses?"

Stefan looked at Roy as if to say "sorry about that" with his eyes. "I needed a little time."

"If we get it back, I'm still going to auction it off provided it brings more than I owe the bank," Roy said a little too loudly over the hum of the rear engine.

"I'm starting to think it's worth north of two million now," Stefan said. "Who knows, it might bring ten million."

"I wish," Roy remarked instantly.

Stefan parked the Porsche near a four-story apartment building at The Fitzhugh at Fairley Farm in Lexington. The first two floors of the structure were alternating patches of cream and burnt-orange brick, and the top two floors were gray metal panels running vertically, broken up by porches and railings. The two men entered the building through a breezeway, searching for Unit 104. When the door swung open, Stefan's mother appeared, looking rather sheepish. "Hello, Mother. May we come in?" He gave her an affectionate hug.

"Mrs. Engel," Roy spoke as he walked past her into the apartment. The unit had oversized windows and expensive, rough-hewn plank flooring. A small section of the wall was weathered barn siding. The tack-room style furniture had the feel of a working horse farm. The kitchen, however, was fit for a Vanderbilt hideaway. "Nice place you have here, ma'am."

"Is something wrong?" she asked.

"Well, I'm not going to ask whether it was you or Dad that switched the car out, but I have to have it back. It legally belongs to this man." He put his hand on Roy's shoulder.

"Your father must have done it. I don't know where the car is."

"Come now, Mother. I know you better than that. There's no way you left Maysville without the Type 64 in tow." Stefan leaned forward in his seat and wove his fingers together.

"I know your father intended to swap it out, but I don't know if he did or not."

Stefan got up and walked into the kitchen. He leaned on the marble countertop and said, "What's it going to take, Mother, for you to tell me where it is?"

"You don't have much to offer. You and Niko are broke," she replied with mild disdain.

"I've got one thing that's worth more than the car, and you know what it is."

"So, you're willing to part with it to clean up Roy's business? Mighty magnanimous of you," she stated in a mocking tone.

"It's the right thing to do," he replied. "I've got what you want in the trunk of my car out there. I'll have Roy hold it here in your apartment while I retrieve the car. So, where is it?"

"I trust you. The keys are in that drawer you're leaning over. The car is in the garage across the street. Spot D thirty-one. There's a cover on it." Stefan left Roy there to make small talk.

When Stefan returned, he had the painting in his hand. *Woman Dancing* by Degas. Phoebe Engel ran to it and blurted, "Look how beautiful it is! Good riddance to that damn car. I disliked it almost as much as I did your father." She grabbed the picture and propped it on the barn siding. That's where she'd hang it, she thought.

Roy asked Stefan how much the painting was worth when they got outside. He said in an offhand way, "More than that piece-of-crap car."

"Then why'd you do the swap? I would have taken the painting instead of the car," Roy admitted.

"Because the painting I just gave her is a forgery."

Roy stepped away from him, and muttered, "Who screws over his own mother?"

"She's not going to sell it. She'll never know the difference. You want to drive your car back?" He handed Roy the keys. They both gazed at the art-deco machine and wondered what the big deal was.

The 38/43 brought $3,815,600 at auction. Tonya told Roy to give Stefan and Niko $1,000,000 of it.

He took it to them in cash.

FLOTSAM AND JETSAM ON THE SEA OF LIFE

The card room at Elysian Fields Country Club in Pewee Valley, Kentucky, gushed with raillery and ripostes on a suffocating Saturday afternoon in late August. It was way too hot to play golf. The serious gamblers were off the course and in the clubhouse looking for some action. The club's best gin player, Boris Piersall, had a high-stakes game going with a man that couldn't afford to be in it.

At the other end of the room, Charlie Cochran took the cellophane off a red pack, separated the jokers, did a quick count to confirm there were fifty-two left, and then fanned the glossy pasteboards out on the heavily varnished oak table. He moved the blue deck that had already been culled aside and swept the empty boxes, wrappers, and useless cards into the wire basket at his feet.

Raleigh Frick, who sat perpendicular to Cochran, stated the rules. "Hollywood. Games are to one-fifty. Twenty-five for gin, twenty-five for an insult. Knock with ten or under. Hand goes dead at two undrawn cards. Winner deals eleven. How much are we playing for?" Notorious gambling was against club rules and Kentucky law, but those impositions were largely ignored.

"A thousand a street," Cochran said softly. He pulled a card and turned over a ten, besting Frick's eight.

Frick shuffled the red cards seven times and presented them to be cut while Cochran prepared the blue deck. Frick made polite conversation as he casually dispatched the hand. "I've never seen you around here before. Did you just join the club?"

Cochran intently watched Frick arrange his cards. He left his own in the order they were dealt. "Yes," he replied nonchalantly.

"Well, thanks for agreeing to a game. Good luck."

Playing for a neighborhood softball team five years ago, Charlie Cochran was running out a grounder hit to the second basemen when the throw to first hit him in the forehead and knocked him unconscious. Charlie had been nothing more than flotsam and jetsam on the sea of life until that moment. He woke up a week later with an expanded mental capacity that he immediately began using to his advantage at the card table. He traveled around to hit casinos for little amounts here and there, but got the greatest satisfaction out of whipping accomplished gin players at private clubs.

Charlie discarded to start play. He had a good idea what was in both Raleigh's hand and the deck by the time the third card had been drawn. Forty-seven minutes later, Frick forked over $4,000 because he had gotten blitzed and had to pay double for losing on the third street. The two of them stood up and shook hands. Raleigh admitted, "You're a hell of a player. I'll need a lot of luck to beat you." Charlie said nothing and strolled to the bar, where he ordered a Maker's Mark and water on ice.

Darla Surratt deliberately pushed the paperwork for the safe-deposit box that she had just rented for $500 back across the glass-topped desk. The weary bank clerk comported himself as though this kind of work was beneath him. After all, he had a finance degree from a good college. "Could you make three copies of that for me?" she asked pleasantly.

"Sure." He dropped the safe-deposit master key on the desk, stood up with the documents, and padded to the copy machine. Darla quietly took a disc of carpenter's wood filler out of her purse, putting it on her lap under the folds of her dress, and carefully pressed the key into it to get a perfect impression out of the camera's view.

After Darla walked out of the bank, Raleigh Frick rose to his feet in the waiting area holding a bag, and told the clerk who was now standing in the lobby that he wanted to put some valuables in his box. The clerk went to retrieve the master key, studied the bag, and made Raleigh sign in before escorting him into the secure room.

Raleigh sidetracked the clerk keying open the box by saying, "Have you ever seen a Saint-Gaudens twenty-dollar gold coin?" He uncinched the bag to retrieve one and swiveled it back and forth in his hand. The clerk eyed it twice with mild interest. "I just bought two hundred of them. Don't trust the stock market these days. With all the government debt, paper money isn't going to be worth much either if things get bad."

"That wouldn't be good for our business," responded the clerk in a slightly sarcastic tone. He swung open the little door and jiggled the master key to remove it from the keyhole. "Take the box into the anteroom over there and call me when you want to lock it up." The clerk waited patiently for Frick to carry the army-green, flip-top metal container out, and then closed the black-iron gate behind them, blocking access to the secure room. Frick, when ready to leave the vault, made sure the clerk saw that the bag once carrying gold coins had been emptied. Frick left the bank with a cheerful head nod.

The weather changed for the good by Saturday before Labor Day. The humidity had dissipated nicely, and the light air made it seem like a crisp fall day. Raleigh saw Charlie Cochran at the bar and scurried over to chat with him. "Hey, how's it going?"

"Fine. Can I buy you a drink?" Cochran asked.

"No, thanks. I'm playing gin in a few minutes. Got any tips?"

"Yeah. Don't arrange your hand so an opponent can figure out what you have."

"Ah, so that's how you beat me," Frick resolved.

"That's part of it," Cochran confirmed. "The rest is simple math and luck."

Cochran followed Frick to the table and sat next to the popcorn machine to see if anyone in the room needed a game or partner. A waitress from the club restaurant wearing a name tag that read "Darla" walked up to Frick, handed him a pair of flat, shiny keys, and said, "Fifteen eleven." He accepted them in his hand without looking up or speaking. Cochran's mind began processing the event at a mile a minute.

The Friday morning after Labor Day, Charlie saw the snippet in the newspaper that read:

Yesterday, the Branch Manager at Pierpont Bank & Trust noticed water dripping into the vault area dedicated to safe-deposit boxes. Upon investigation, bank personnel determined that rain had leaked through a cutout made in the roof by a would-be burglar. There was no way to be sure when the break-in attempt occurred. None of the safe-deposit boxes showed signs of being tampered with. The bank was taking steps to fortify the security of the vault roof.

A stream of customers stormed *Pierpont* on Friday afternoon to check on their belongings. The clerk had to escort them in and out of the vault area one at a time. Most people, including Darla Surratt, cleaned out their boxes and grumbled as they left. When it was Raleigh Frick's turn to enter the secure room, he stood impatiently by his box as the aggravated clerk keyed open the door again. Frick slid the container out, shook it, and flipped up the lid in a panic. "Where's my gold?" he growled. Beads of sweat formed on the clerk's forehead. "I paid five hundred for this box, and the agreement says you're liable for the contents up to five hundred times the rent. I expect the bank to pay me at least two hundred and fifty thousand for this loss. You should really reimburse me for the full value of the gold that's gone, which is three hundred thousand." Frick dropped the empty box in the anteroom with a clang and marched in the direction of the branch manager's office.

An hour later, Charlie Cochran peeked in the restaurant at Elysian Fields. Odoriferous corned beef and cabbage were featured at the buffet under a bright heat lamp. He saw the "Darla" woman standing over Raleigh Frick and Boris Piersall at a four-top in the corner. They were gabbing about something and laughing heartily. Chatter from other customers made it hard to hear what the conversation was about.

Charlie's mind rolled through the likely scenarios until he came to the one he liked best. He rushed down to the computer used for posting golf scores that was in the men's locker room to Google a website that sold information on criminal backgrounds. Boris Piersall had been arrested for insurance fraud eight years ago, but was never convicted. Cochran pondered that while he erased the search history. He heard an angry creak from the computer chair as he shoved it back and stood up to dart outside.

Charlie surveyed the car lot and deduced where the employees parked behind a row of dense hedges that blocked vehicles from being seen from inside the white-painted, brick clubhouse. Food smells wafted in spurts through the lot when the breeze kicked up. He studied the eleven cars and narrowed down the possibilities to three of them. Charlie scanned the area carefully to make sure no one saw him there. He looked in the window of the sedan near the hedgerow, tried the door, and found it unlocked. He reached in and pushed a button to unlock the trunk.

Ten minutes later, Cochran walked over to Raleigh Frick, who was still sitting with Piersall at the table in the dining room, and said, "You up for a gin game?"

Frick focused his eyes suspiciously on Charlie and replied, "Have you met Boris?" He cast a hand in Piersall's direction. "You might get a game with him."

"We've met," Charlie answered. He acknowledged Piersall with a nod. Boris could have been a young version of Wilfred Brimley if he added thirty pounds and traded the glasses he wore that had massive black frames and stems for a pair of wire rims.

"What's your upper limit per street?" Boris displayed a come-on phizog.

"Oh, I'd say fifty thousand."

"Make it seventy-five, and we'll go in the card room and see which way the wind blows."

"Did you bring a personal check, or do you have that kind of cash on the premises?"

That galled Boris, so he fired back, "Pretty cocky, aren't you? I'll take your personal check if the wind blows the other way, and it always does. I've never lost at this club."

"Good for you. I've got my checkbook right here." Charlie patted the right-front side of his sport coat with his left hand.

"Are you sure you want to do this?" Boris squinted at him through his ridiculous eyewear.

"Why, certainly. Let's go work up the decks." The three men moved to the card room, Darla following close behind. Word spread around the club like wildfire that a big-money game was underway, and it didn't take long for small crowds to form at the backs of both players.

The first two streets were woefully uneventful. Cochran took them easily, with little fanfare. Boris was mad as a hornet, but worked as hard as he could not to let it show. He had never been beaten like that by anybody. The only people who stayed around to watch the third street were Raleigh Frick and Darla Surratt, and they seemed damned nervous. The last game had gotten interesting, not only because it was the difference between Piersall losing $75,000 or $300,000, but due to the odd nature of the scores. Boris sat on 149, Charlie at 121.

Two cards were left to be drawn before the hand would be dead. The players hadn't looked directly at one another for fifteen minutes. Boris took off his glasses and rubbed his eyes in preparation for the homestretch. His hand held three kings, three sevens, three fives, and the nine of hearts as a defensive play. Charlie had a ten-jack-queen-king heart run, five-six-seven-eight spade run, and two aces. Both men were certain that an ace of spades, four of diamonds, six of clubs, and ten of diamonds were among the two live and two dead cards left in the deck.

Boris Piersall knew that if he drew the ace, he could discard the nine of hearts and knock with one to catch Charlie with two, giving him the one point he needed to win the game. The four of diamonds came up on the draw. Boris exhaled and discarded the nine in disgust. That's when he made his mistake. He should have knocked with four, absorbed the net two loss, and twenty-five insult points to live to fight another hand, but he didn't. Cochran smiled. He knew he would either win the game on the final draw or get at least two points and play another hand after he knocked.

Charlie hesitated for a moment, then took the palm of his left hand and ran it up his forehead. He turned over the last live card, the ace of spades, like it was a hot potato. He discarded the five of spades and declared, "Gin." Charlie Cochran tucked the ace in his hand, fanned the cards, and laid them in the middle of the table. The twenty-nine-point win ran his score up to exactly 150. That was game, set, and match.

Piersall huffed with exasperation and begrudgingly wrote out a check for $300,000. Cochran snatched it up as he rose from his seat to head out of the club.

Boris, Darla, and Raleigh left the card room together after a few moments of silence. They moved with despair toward the employee parking lot, and on the way, Boris stopped and spat, "How did that son of a bitch do that? I'm going to let the check bounce and make him sue me for the money."

When the three of them got to Darla's car, she said, "Can't be helped. Do you want to take your third of the two fifty in coins now, or do you want to wait until he gets the cash from the bank? I don't know if someone can trace the gold if you try to sell it to somebody or not."

Frick said, "I'd rather he wait until I get the money."

"I want the gold coins." Piersall demanded. "I'm going to quit this club and join another one." Frick turned his back on the group. Darla pressed her key fob to open the trunk.

When she got to the rear of her car, she raised the lid and uttered too loudly, "It's not here!" The two men jumped around to where Darla stood and were stunned by the vacancy of the trunk.

"I'm going to kill that Cochran," Boris murmured.

Saturdays were the busiest days at Elysian Fields Country Club. Virtually every member showed up for golf, gambling, crosstalk, libations, or victuals. The place could be taken for a funeral home from the outside if it weren't for the Porsches, Jaguars, and Bentleys that dotted the car park. Inside, Charlie Cochran sat in the lobby before noon in the hope that Raleigh Frick would come through the door. When he did, Charlie spoke up, "Hey, Raleigh. Care to catch a bite of lunch?"

"I guess so," he said despondently.

They took a seat at a two-top in the corner of the restaurant, away from the other tables. The noise coming from the bar area camouflaged their conversation. Charlie said, "I want you to hear something." He sat a smartphone on the table and pressed play. The video was dark, but the sound of the voices was as clear as a bell. It was a recording of what was said by Darla, Raleigh, and Boris around her car last night.

"What? Were you hiding in the bushes recording us?"

"Don't get any wise ideas about grabbing this. It isn't the only copy." Cochran leaned back in his chair and suddenly looked very sinister to Raleigh.

"So, what do you want?"

"This goes to the bank unless you do two things. Tell Boris to make good on the three hundred thousand dollar check I'm holding, and give me a quarter of the two hundred fifty thousand that's coming your way soon."

"You don't know what you're talking about."

"Well, let me spell it out for you. The three of you trumped up this insurance fraud. You put the gold in your box. Darla stole a master key, and Boris cut a hole in the roof of the bank and moved the gold from your box to Darla's. She cleaned out her box, and you tapped the bank for your phony loss. Is that pretty close?"

"You know, Cochran, you're skating on thin ice here, partner. You might turn up missing one of these days."

Charlie ignored that and continued on, "What I can't quite figure out is why Piersall didn't just pull the money out of your box and take it with him when he broke in. I think he was hedging his bet. If there happened to be security cameras inside or out, the masked man breaking in wouldn't be seen stealing from the bank or carrying anything through the parking lot. He also knew that if something went wrong, he could pin the scam on you and Darla. I'd watch my back around that guy if I were you."

"Watch who?" Charlie looked over his shoulder to see Boris Piersall standing there with clenched fists. Raleigh felt relief.

"You, my friend. I wouldn't trust you further than I could throw you. What are you doing here?" Cochran didn't appear to be afraid of Piersall.

"I brought in my letter of resignation from the club, thanks to you. Are you some kind of savant? I've spent my life learning how to remember cards and play the odds."

"Boris, there's always somebody better." Charlie grabbed his phone, stood up, and pushed Boris aside to step away from the table. He turned around and said, "Have Raleigh here tell you what the deal is."

When Cochran reached his Maserati in the parking lot, he saw Boris coming toward him yelling his name. "What do you want?" Charlie questioned.

Boris loped up to him and came to a halt at the front of the car. He replied savagely, "The gold and my check back. I plan on teaching you a lesson." He arced around aggressively to face Charlie and grabbed him by the throat. Charlie kicked him and tried to shove him down to no avail. That's when Boris landed a haymaker to the forehead that sent Cochran to the ground in a heap. Other men in the parking lot saw what was going on and sprinted over to pull Piersall off.

When Charlie Cochran came to, his card smarts were gone. He tried to play golf matches for money, but his reputation in the card room scared everybody away. So, sadly, he returned to being the flotsam and jetsam on the sea of life that he had once been.

There's a Train a Comin'

The Anderson brothers—Kenneth, Anthony, and Joshua—had all been married at least twice. They were certifiably bad husbands, and respectable women knew instinctively to stay away from them. As Wall Street hedge fund managers, they were "large and in charge." Their interest in brown liquor, after grueling days at the office, heightened as the bourbon craze swept through New York. Having bought up nearly every hundred-dollar shot of Pappy Van Winkle in the city, they got the bright idea to make their own great whiskey. Craft distilleries were popping up like weeds, and the Anderson brothers were arrogant enough to believe that producing their own elite brand was actually doable.

Years later, on a bleak Thursday afternoon in February, Bradford Hollingsworth wheeled his metallic-gold Mercedes SUV into the empty lot at High Bridge. The low ceiling of stratus clouds and hoar frost on the leafless bushes brought to mind a black-and-white movie with one glaring contradiction: the massive, mocha railroad bridge, which was the main attraction at the park, had the feel of the Eiffel Tower laying on its side. Kenny Anderson opened the passenger door and eased his feet gingerly onto the icy pavement. "So, this is it," he brayed for the amusement of his younger brothers in the back seat.

Hollingsworth answered, "Pretty spooky looking, don't you think? Runs twice a day." The recherché train bridge was something of an engineering marvel, still in operation today, awesome for its tremendous height and span across the Kentucky River cataract.

"I'll say," said Kenny as he reclaimed his seat in the vehicle.

Tony mused, "Wonder if the word *high* in the name of our bourbon will have the connotation of drunkenness?"

"No," Bradford assured him. "One of the best-selling cheap bourbons of the twentieth century was called Ten High."

Bradford Hollingsworth had been the man chosen by the brothers to make their vision a reality. He had found a collapsed, abandoned barrel warehouse five years ago on Shakertown Road, between Shaker Village and Burgin, Kentucky, where he salvaged all the timber and siding to construct a small distillery right there on the site along with a storage room to age the barrels. The trestle and tracks that connected the train to High Bridge ran along the south edge of the property. It took a year to bring the operation online at a price tag of two million dollars, cheerfully paid for by the Andersons.

The first batch of bourbon was ready to go in the bottle and back to New York. Hollingsworth used smaller barrels and accelerated aging techniques from the day the "white dog" came off the still, giving the whiskey the taste of a twenty-year-old product, and to bottle it without an age footnote on the label, the juice had been in the barrel for the required four years.

Josh offered, "I don't care about the name. It's all about how it tastes, baby." He flickered a madcap expression, and then lapsed back into his normal state of ennui.

Hollingsworth said, "I've set everything up for a tasting in the barrelhouse at seven o'clock."

The tires of the Mercedes slipped intermittently on the pavement as the men drove toward the Harrodsburg Road car bridge that crossed the Kentucky River. The limestone cliffs were dappled with icicles from water that had oozed through the rocks. Tony shivered spontaneously in the back seat as the light of day gave way to darkness. He glanced at the speedometer before putting his head back and closing his eyes. This certainly *ain't* New York, he thought.

Since it was the shortest route to the thermostat, Pastor John Hocknell used the side door to enter the 200-year old, one-room Shadrack Quaker Church next to the distillery. He carefully turned the dial from fifty to seventy as he took out a handkerchief to blow his nose, which had begun to tickle from the cold. The Lee sisters would be arriving in thirty minutes, a little before seven o'clock, to practice the number they would sing on Sunday, as they had done as long as Hocknell could remember, and he wanted them to be as comfortable as possible in the musty, old, dilapidated church. He left the side door unlocked, returned to his car, cranked up the heater fan, and drove through the trestle in the direction of Burgin.

Ann was the oldest and meanest of the Lee sisters. Nancy had the best personality, and Mildred was afraid of her own shadow. They made it a habit of showing up to singing practice fifteen minutes early out of respect for each other's time. Not one of them had ever been late, but this Thursday was different. Ann had overslept from an unusually deep nap she took, Nancy didn't recognize that her kitchen clock had stopped at 6:35, and Mildred's car didn't start right away.

Hollingsworth parked the Mercedes near the entrance to the High Bridge Distillery at 6:55. The four men briskly stepped inside to get out of the frigid air, turned on the lights to inspect the still area for a few minutes, and then opened the formidable oak door that led into the barrelhouse. There were four glasses and a copper tube for scooping liquid called a whiskey thief perched on an oak-stave cocktail table that stood at the four-way intersection of the dark aisles. Josh said, "You've done a marvelous job with the place, Brad. We'll really know how well you've done when we get a taste." Kenny and Tony nodded and grinned in anticipation as they gathered around.

Hollingsworth took the mallet hanging on a nail in the corner post and banged on the barrel until the bung loosened and popped out. The smoky caramel smell of booze pervaded the dead-air space they were in like pleasant fumes from a bakery. He stuck the whiskey thief in the barrel and extracted enough to fill the four glasses. Kenny sloshed the liquid around, sniffed it, and took a swig. "Oh man, this is the best stuff I've ever tasted. We've done it!" He raised his glass in a formal toast to the group. The other men did the same as Kenny, gazing afterward at their hands as if they held liquid gold.

At 7:12, Ann Lee approached the church from the south, slowing down in disbelief when she saw the headlights of both Nancy and Mildred's cars driving toward her from the north. "What are the chances that all three of us would be twelve minutes late on the same day?" she asked herself. The answer was zero. At that very second, the church exploded in a horrific ball of fire. The air piston made her car sway viciously. Ann became disoriented and veered off the road into the mouth of the parking lot at High Bridge Distillery.

Nancy and Mildred pulled in next to her, both launching out of their cars at the same time in a paroxysm of shock. Mildred cried out, "Look, the distillery building has collapsed on one side and the fire is spreading!" She noticed the Mercedes, pointed at the door in front of it, and screamed, "There's somebody in there!"

The stunning blast, a gust of air, and creaking timbers damn near stopped the hearts of the men in the barrelhouse. Befuddled collectively, they staggered to regain their balance. The glasses they had been holding had flown into the aisle that led out. The huge oak door had swung completely open from the air pressure, bounced off the wall, and slammed shut from the recoil. Hollingsworth studied the disfigured rows of barrels that were leaning inward. He could see the fire through the hole in the wall. Whiskey trickled down onto the floor at an alarming rate. Smoke gathered in the aisles, and then the lights went out. Kenny started beating on the door, yelling, "Help!"

The three sisters heard the sirens of the fire trucks off in the distance. The roof and walls of the church collapsed, tamping down the blaze, and dimming the orange light it emitted. The adjacent wall at the distillery was going in the other direction as the fire over there had brightened considerably.

Against their better judgment, the sisters ran into the distillery only to hear someone pounding, coughing, and bellowing for help on the other side of the wall in the back. When they un-latched the big door, the smoky air in the aisle, acting as a venturi, blew it open, the men out, and the women onto the ground. The brothers landed on top of the women, coinci-dentally matched up correctly by age. Anne, Nancy, and Mildred were incensed, in a good sort of way.

The firemen assessed the situation quickly and put all of their effort into keeping the barrelhouse from exploding, which they were able to do over the next hour. The old Quaker church that should have been condemned years ago finally succumbed to its long-overdue death. The damage to the distillery, although con-siderable, could be repaired.

Kenny turned to the sisters and said, "You saved our lives. How can we repay you?"

Ann replied somberly, "It was divine intervention. We were sup-posed to be in the church right now. You can repay Him." She pointed upward and looked toward the sky.

Nancy spoke up, "There is one way I can think of. You can come to our service on Sunday to hear us sing. I guess we'll have to rent the church hall at Shaker Village. The acoustics are pretty good in there. We always appreciate contributions when the plate is passed."

Tony asked, "Did you have insurance on the place?"

"A little. The building wasn't worth much," Mildred said.

Josh allowed, "We'll be here tomorrow sorting through this mess. We're staying at Shaker Village ourselves. I hope we can make your Sunday service to hear you sing. We fly back to New York in the afternoon." He looked to his brothers for affirmation of the plan he espoused but received none. It was nearly midnight when Hollingsworth dropped the Andersons off at their ascetic rooms.

Clear skies and the beaming sun on Friday morning presented a stark picture of the church's burnt wreckage. The once entirely virgin-timber structure had clearly become a tinderbox on borrowed time. The fire investigators and forensic team bumbled around for several hours in the charred mess with only a low level of enthusiasm, searching for anything suspicious or out of the ordinary. One of the technicians noticed something that he brought to the attention of the lead investigator. The entire team gathered around to discuss what they had found.

The shrill whistle could be heard in the distance as the train crossed High Bridge at a little after two o'clock on Friday afternoon. The click-clack got louder as the juggernaut approached the edge of the distillery property. Bradford Hollingsworth stopped working for a few seconds to count the rusted freight cars coupled behind the green, aerodynamic engine. His trance broke and he returned to loading the barrels of whiskey that were still intact onto the semi that had been called in. After the train passed out of earshot, he confirmed to Kenny, "I'll send these over to the bottling plant in Taylorsville and we'll get as much out of them as we can. In a couple of weeks, we'll be back in business."

The three sisters stood outside of the rooms the Andersons were sleeping in at eight a.m. sharp on Saturday morning. They coordinated with each other to synchronize the door knocks. "Rise and shine," Nancy proclaimed. "We have a big day planned for you men."

It was over a minute before all three sleepyheads stood in their open doorways. The warm, dead air in the place smelled of old wooden floors and furniture. A shaft of sunlight with roiling motes of dust made Tony raise his hand to cover his eyes. Josh, the most alert of the group, wanted to know, "What exactly do you have in mind?" He felt lonesome and homesick from the lack of city noise, or any noise at all for that matter.

"Kentucky hospitality. We're going to take some of that city slicker out of you today," Ann replied.

Tony said, "Give us twenty minutes, and we'll meet you in the restaurant."

The sisters chose a picnic-style table that seated six. They left it up to the brothers to pick a partner like at a square dance party. Kenny legged over the bench seat and sat across from Ann. Tony slid in to face Nancy, and Mildred looked away when Josh ogled her as he seated himself. Ann said, "Here, try some of these deep-fried biscuits and apple butter. They'll fix you right up."

Josh interrupted her in a serious tone, "Are you girls trying to proselytize us?"

"Certainly not. If you fellows want to be heathens, that's your business," Nancy said. The Anderson brothers went on to spend the most enjoyable day of their lives despite the cold weather, thanks to the country charm of the Lee sisters, who did have ulterior motives.

Members filed into the rented hall on Sunday morning as if nothing had happened to the razed church building up the road. The men wore drab coats and ties that they must've had for better than ten years. The women wore plain skirts and Pentecostal hairdos. A rented organ sat angled in a back corner of the room and the bass guitar leaned on a stand next to it. The Anderson brothers looked like monkeys in their thousand-dollar suits and hundred-dollar ties, but they didn't care much, nor did the parishioners.

When it came time for the Lee sisters to sing, the ladies made their way to the dais and clustered around the microphone. Ann wore a violet dress, Nancy's was Dutch blue, and Mildred had on a baby-blue flared thing. Ann announced to the congregation,

"We want to dedicate this number to our guests, the Andersons, who are seated right over there." She pointed them out and smiled pleasantly. The organist and bassist played a torturous gospel introduction, and when the Lee sisters broke into "People Get Ready," the hairs on the back of the necks of the Anderson boys stood on end. The trio proclaimed in song that "there's a train a comin'" and to get on board.

The applause from the crowd was surprisingly raucous. Kenny, Tony, and Joshua popped out of their seats energetically as tears streamed down their faces. When the collection plate came by, Joshua dropped a check in it.

After the service, Kenny congratulated Ann on the beautiful spiritual. He questioned her, "Is everything all right?"

"Not really. This morning, the police called my house and asked if I thought anyone was trying to kill me or one of my sisters."

"What?"

"He said that a wire connection had been found that opened a gas valve when the thermostat was turned up. It allowed gas to build up under the floor until it eventually exploded. Someone rigged the church to blow up."

Kenny put one hand under an elbow, leaned back against the wall, and tapped his toes. He cogitated for a moment, then said, "Ann, can you do me a favor? I need to find some bolt cutters and a hammer, and get a ride over to Taylorsville."

"Mildred has cutters in her shed. I can run you over there."

Kenny easily spotted the semi parked outside the bottling plant. He deftly took the bolt cutters and sheared off the padlock to gain entry to the trailer. Ann watched him tip one of the barrels over and hammer it to loosen the bung. Kenny rolled the barrel until some of the whiskey spilled into a Styrofoam cup. It tasted nothing like the whiskey he and his brothers had sampled on Thursday evening.

At one thirty, the brothers Anderson and sisters Lee stood in the glass vestibule of the main building at Shaker Village to shield against the relentless cold, waiting for the men to be picked up by Brad Hollingsworth. Tony looked at his watch and asked, "What's going on? He should have been here by now."

Kenny turned to Ann and looked in her eyes. "We need one more favor. Can you girls take us to High Bridge right now?"

"Mildred, pull your car up. I'll run and get mine."

Kenny sprinted on the dry pavement over to the upper portion of the bridge when he spotted the man standing out a ways on the shimmering railroad tracks. "Stop!" Hollingsworth barked in desperation. "Don't come out here or I'll jump!"

"Just tell me one thing. Were you planning on killing us all at the distillery, including yourself?" Kenny heard the first noises of the train steaming toward the bridge. The cold crosswinds blew in erratic, ominous gusts.

"No. I intended to go back to the church later that evening to put things in motion. Someone must've turned the thermostat up earlier, which I hadn't counted on. It would have been better for me if we would've been killed." His voice trailed off despondently.

"Brad, we forgive you, man. Come off the bridge now. We can work this out." The other five people gathered around Kenny for moral support. The whistle of the locomotive blared out vehemently as it got closer. Tony stepped forward as if he intended to chase after Hollingsworth.

"Don't! I'll jump. I'm not kidding." The sibilant sound of the spinning wheels and chugging of the engine suddenly drowned the conversation. The Andersons and Lees backed away from the tracks when the engineer laid on the whistle and didn't let up. As the train barreled onto the bridge, Hollingsworth continued to stand defiantly on the tracks. Then the whistle stopped.

After the train had completely cleared the bridge, everyone ran out to where Hollingsworth was last seen. There was no trace of him.

In early September, later that year, three couples stood at the altar of the new Shadrack Quaker Church built on the site of the one that had burned down. The dazzling sun radiated through the stained glass window that had been salvaged from an old church in New York City and installed as the main feature of the apse in the new church.

The wedding reception for the three married couples was all set up at the High Bridge Distillery next door. The Anderson brothers hoped that all of the parishioners would be in attendance.

NAOMI FROM BORNEO

HARZUL LIM

On a partly sunny Saturday in early April, spring hadn't yet sprung at Keeneland horse track in Lexington, Kentucky. The raw air that whisked around made the forty-six degrees feel inopportunely cold to the boisterous, well-dressed crowd. Neutron Star ambled along with an unpretentious four-beat gait, robotically bobbing his head up and down to maintain his balance. The walker led him into the paddock area through the gap in the hedges next to the mammoth sycamore tree that would soon be laden with thousands of leaves the size of dinner plates.

Neutron Star stopped long enough to allow his trainer, Lionel Crawford, to give the tiny jockey a leg up. Crawford's only words of advice were, "Just don't fall off." The horse swung his head around to cast an angry eye in the direction of the trainer as though he understood perfectly what had been said.

Encik Harzul Lim, one of the owners of Neutron Star, fidgeted comically as he stood next to the trainer on the grassy lawn inside the paddock ring. The nippy breeze compelled him to put his hands on his ears to warm them. He asked nervously, "Does he look alright?"

"Better than alright. He looks fantastic," Crawford assured him. They both watched as the horses were sent through the tunnel out to the track. The shaved checkerboard on *Star's* left-rear hip was the last thing the two men saw before taking the elevator up to a fourth-floor box.

Lim was a short, swarthy man of Malaysian and Chinese descent. He lived in Seria, Brunei, on the island of Borneo. He worked in an administrative capacity for the monarchy, which meant he knew how to skillfully embezzle money from the Wealth Agency, Investment Agency, and well-heeled aristocrats who could lose track of billions without batting an eye.

Wildcatters struck oil in Brunei in 1929, and since then, money has gushed into the pockets of the royal family. Siphoning off a million here or there was as easy as clubbing baby seals. Lim used some of what he swiped to invest in an expensive American racehorse that had become a Kentucky Derby hopeful. Neutron Star needed to win the race that Crawford had dropped him into that day if he was going to get an invitation to run on the first Saturday in May.

Lionel Crawford's reputation was that of a miracle worker. He'd been suspended numerous times for trying every trick in the book to plus up the performances of horses he trained. Buzzers, cocktails, drugs, liniments—you name it—he'd been fined for it. He had no concerns with Lim's animal, though. The horse trained like a champion, was fast as hell, and wasn't even on Lasix. Crawford had been warned that one more suspension for wrongdoing, and he would be banned from horse racing for life.

Neutron Star looked majestic barreling down the homestretch eight lengths ahead of the rest of the pack. "You did it!" Lim bellowed as he pawed at the trainer like a pet that needed to go out.

Lionel Crawford responded, "Yes, we did." He'd been there before.

NAOMI BARR

Naomi Barr, originally from Bardstown, the epicenter of Kentucky bourbon, graduated from nearby Centre College only a few short years ago. She'd been a bit-part player in the theater of life until deciding to become a *feng shui* consultant. There weren't any required certifications, so she could sell a line of crap on the subject to anybody that would listen.

She built a snazzy website and waited for cyber customers to walk through the door. Remarkably, one did, a member of the royal family of Brunei. She moved her business to Borneo and began flying all over the world to stylize the family's plummy properties, one of which happened to be northwest of Keeneland, right up the road from Lionel Crawford's home office.

The Sunday morning after Neutron Star's big win, Crawford sat in the track kitchen at Keeneland, holding court, accepting congratulations from those who knew him. He filled a paper cup with hot coffee after breakfast and climbed into his beat-up farm truck to drive up the hill to the barn. Steam radiated off *Star* as he was being brushed down by the groom. Crawford talked briefly with the exercise rider, and a few minutes later, wheeled over to Pisgah Road to head for home. He espied the woman waving vigorously at him from a distance. She was tall, curvy, and had a roundish head with a black haircut cropped like a motorcycle helmet.

"What seems to be the problem, ma'am?"

"Look at that tire. It's almost flat."

"Jump in. We'll go up to my place and get a pump." She seemed hesitant to accept his invitation. "I only live a few hundred yards from here."

The woman introduced herself. Crawford gave his name in response. She said, "I live in Borneo. I'm here to decorate that house owned by a royal family member in Brunei." She looked over her shoulder at the brick two-story that sat back from the road. "The place has a solid-gold toilet in it, if you can believe that," she revealed.

He chuckled and replied, "Small world. I train a horse for a guy from Brunei." Naomi shuddered ever so slightly, and her eyes widened.

Crawford turned into the rutted path at his house and got out of the truck to retrieve an air pump from the garage. They went back to her car, and he methodically blew up the flat tire and remarked when she got behind the wheel, "I'd get that checked out to make sure you haven't picked up a nail. You know where I live if you need any more help." She nodded compliantly as she eased out onto the road while rolling up the car window to wall off the cold air.

A startling knock on Crawford's door a few hours later woke him from his customary Sunday afternoon nap on the couch. He rubbed his eyes, sat up, and went in sock feet to see who was there. Naomi Barr stood on the stoop with the opposite of a come-hither look. "Well, there was a nail in the tire, and I got ripped off by a brute that complained about having to fix it on Sunday."

"I'm sorry to hear that. You collecting charitable donations?"

"Funny." The huffy attitude she fought to hold onto drained out of her.

Crawford swept his hand toward the entrance hall. "Won't you come in?"

She entered, turned around, and said, "You need to get rid of that table. The door should open as wide as possible to let in the energy, money, and possibilities. I'm a *feng shui* consultant."

"Anything else wrong?"

"Yeah, that blank wall will never do. The first thing you should see when you walk in must bring you joy. Put a colorful painting or something there."

"How about a picture of you?" he commented to derail her.

"You're making fun of me," she responded cynically.

"No, I'm not. I'm a consultant myself. I train horses. You have to use neurolinguistics on them."

"I'm not a horse," she argued.

"It works on humans," he confirmed with confidence. Naomi stayed around for another two hours, putting the *feng shui* hammer down on his whole house. They exchanged phone numbers when she announced her imminent departure. He wondered what the hell was going on.

NEUTRON STAR

Crawford's cell phone rang abruptly on Monday afternoon. "You been fending off the press this morning?" he asked Harzul. There was a long silence on the other end.

"I just got a call from the racing board. Neutron Star failed the drug test. He had too much scopolamine in his blood."

"What?"

"Four hundred nanograms per milliliter. They've banned him from racing for sixty days."

"Damn it. Somebody must have laced his feed." Crawford twisted around to look at the horse. "They'll blame me for this and take my license. I'll try to figure out how it happened. Maybe we can get the test overturned." He looked again, sadly, at Neutron Star, who turned his head to stare back at him.

"Will money do anything?"

"I don't think so." Crawford cut the line and waved the groom over. He asked, "When was the last time the feed store came by?"

The groom said, "Friday. They brought two bags."

"How much is left?"

"A little more than a bag."

"Is the full bag unopened?"

"Yes." The groom began walking toward the stall to find it.

Crawford crouched down and grabbed a handful of feed from the open bag and began carefully picking through it. "Don't touch that." He pointed at the unopened one. "I'll have someone come for it." He stood up and placed a return call to Lim. "Harzul, call the racing board back and ask them to send someone out here. The feed store brought bags that have some chopped up jimson weed in them."

When the pickup truck from the test lab arrived hours later, the forlorn trainer explained the situation. The lab techs took pictures and loaded up what was left of the feed.

Lionel Crawford left the barn at six o'clock in a state of abject despair. He drove up to Naomi Barr's house to see if she would join him for dinner and conversation. The two-story had a half-round porch with cream-colored columns in front of a formidable façade of golden-brown, Flemish-bond brickwork. The oversized double-hung windows made the structure look bigger than it actually was. He pounded on one of the yellow double doors that had gaudy, brass kick-plates along the bottom. No answer. He texted her, "Where are you?" No response. He walked around to the rear of the house to see if the back door happened to be unlocked. He turned the knob and yelled her name. Crawford milled around inside for a while, ending up in the master bathroom upstairs. He gawked in disbelief at the solid gold toilet that had to be worth five million dollars.

LIONEL CRAWFORD

Crawford went over to the barn at sunup on Tuesday morning, but returned home after Neutron Star's workout to prepare a Spanish omelet, rasher of bacon, and ramekin of chopped cantaloupe. His coffee was strong enough to float a horseshoe. The first phone call he received came from Naomi Barr.

"I saw you texted me yesterday. I was in Cincinnati looking for artwork."

"No worries. I came by to fetch you for dinner."

"Let's go out tonight. Pick me up at six." Just as she said that, another call was coming in from Lim. He abruptly hung up after saying okay.

"The board said they planned to check bags at the feed store to see if they could find any with jimson weed. Regardless, there is no way the horse will be cleared in time for the Derby."

Crawford said, "They'll keep the failed test confidential. You should tell the selection committee that Neutron Star will be skipping the Derby, and that you want him withdrawn from consideration. If we get him cleared, he can come back and prove himself the rest of the racing season."

Naomi Barr waited out by the road so that Lionel Crawford could scoop her up for their dinner date. Warmer weather had finally arrived, and it seemed as though the greenery along the tree line was growing so fast that you could actually see the leaves bursting forth. The fields of new grass across the road were a rich emerald, reminiscent of Ireland. Crawford's black Lincoln SUV came over the hill slowly and stopped in the street in front of the brick house. "Where are we going?" Naomi asked.

"I got a reservation at Tony's."

"Oh, goody. People have recommended it to me. I usually eat at the Kentucky Castle down the hill on the corner." She had on an off-white pantsuit that accentuated her full figure. He wore dressy blue jeans, a blue button-down shirt, and a clownish blue-and-brown sport coat.

Once seated at the restaurant, he asked her, "Where are you from?"

"I grew up in Bardstown and moved to Borneo when I got the *feng shui* gig with the royal family."

"Did you go to Thomas Nelson or Bardstown High?"

"Nelson." She looked uncomfortable with the question, so she changed the subject. "I Googled you and saw you've cut a few corners in your day."

"Yeah, I did when I was much younger. I'm as pure as the driven snow now." The conversation loosened up after that. They finished the meal and returned to the royal family's house for a nightcap. Both of them had the twenty-three-year-old Pappy Van Winkle that was tucked in the back of the liquor cabinet. The loneliness that Crawford had been carrying around since hearing about the tainted feed finally left him when he returned home at midnight.

News broke on Wednesday afternoon that Neutron Star would not be running in the Kentucky Derby. Crawford spent the rest of the day fielding visits and phone calls from the horse racing press. One reporter asked him point-blank, "Did the horse fail the drug test?"

"I don't have any information on that," he replied with disinterest. Something about Naomi was bothering him.

THE GOLDEN TOILET

When he got home before dinnertime, Crawford guessed Naomi's age and began looking online at the Thomas Nelson High School yearbooks. It didn't take him long to find her picture in one of the senior classes. The hairdo hadn't changed, but her face and eyes certainly looked "dumber" back then. He scanned the rest of the book looking for other photos of her, and then went to the Bardstown High School yearbook to see if she happened to be in any sports pictures. Oddly enough, she popped up in an interesting crowd picture at a football game. He clicked out of the internet and picked up his phone. "Harzul, do you know a woman by the name of Naomi Barr, who lives in Brunei?"

"Yes. She's a decorator for the royal family. She also owns half of Neutron Star."

"You're kidding me."

"No. She's originally from Kentucky, and when she found out I was going to buy a horse, she wanted in on it."

"Well, Naomi's here in town, decorating a house for the royal family right up the road from me. The place has a golden toilet. Come on over here, and we'll surprise her."

Lim arrived in thirty minutes. He asked, "Do you want to get something to eat?"

"Yes. After we visit Naomi." They went down the road in Crawford's SUV and parked at the corner of the brick house. There was no answer again to the loud knock. Lim saw that the door was slightly ajar. He pushed it open deliberately. This time he was the one to yell her name. No answer. They walked through the house and found nothing personal. One thing stood out as both men looked in the master bathroom at the same time. There was an open hole in the floor. The golden toilet was gone.

"Look at that," Lim remarked.

"Come on. I think I know where she is." Crawford veered dangerously into the Kentucky Castle entrance at the corner of Pisgah and Versailles Roads. He talked his way through security and pulled up to the valet station. "Keep this parked right over there. We may be leaving in a hurry. Thanks." They marched into the restaurant together. Naomi was laying cash on the tray that held the bill. Crawford walked up to her and said, "Hi there, did you enjoy your dinner?" She looked at him, then Lim.

Lim said, "What a surprise to see you. Why didn't you let me know you were here?"

Naomi stood and stated, "I was just leaving."

Crawford stepped in front of her and revealed to Lim what he had learned on the internet. "Wait a minute, Harzul. This isn't Naomi Barr. Her name is Brenda Sutton. She's a high-school friend of Naomi's."

"You don't say." Lim feigned shock.

At that moment, the pieces of the puzzle fell into place for Crawford. "So, Brenda, I presume you stay in touch with Naomi. She must have told you about Neutron Star and the golden toilet." He turned his attention to Lim. "And why did you agree to let her impersonate your partner, because of the money? Did you tip her off that I was on to her?" Lim ignored him.

Brenda Sutton said viciously, "Naomi stole the idea of being a *feng shui* consultant from me. Look where she is now. I've got nothing. Why'd it have to be you that helped me with that flat tire? I shouldn't have told you about the toilet." Her head shook spastically.

"Don't," Lim interrupted her. "Let's get out of here." He addressed Crawford, "Would you like in on the deal?"

When they got outside, the van Brenda drove was at the curb. Lim climbed in the passenger's side just before she stepped on the gas. Crawford fell in behind them. Sutton turned right on Pisgah and headed into horse-farm country at full speed. All of a sudden, she stood on the brakes, and the SUV slammed into the back of the van. He heard another bang and saw Lim fall out of the passenger door on his head. He'd been shot.

Sutton took off again, weaving and swaying recklessly. Crawford rolled into the oncoming lane and rammed the careening vehicle with one bold swerve. The van listed unsteadily and whipped back to the center of the road before it fishtailed wildly to the right, into the ditch, where it hit a slave fence and big maple tree with a sickening thud. Crawford jumped out. Sutton was groaning and falling onto the ground. He reached around her through the door and grabbed the gun by the barrel with his handkerchief. He fumbled his phone out of his pocket and called 911.

Crawford found the golden toilet in the back of the wrecked van while he was waiting for the police and ambulance to arrive. Harzul Lim died in less than a week. Brenda Sutton would soon be sent up for theft and murder.

Three months later, the real Naomi from Borneo, who now owned 100 percent of Neutron Star, sat in a box at Saratoga, waiting for the feature to go off. The racing board found jimson weed in other feed bags and cleared the horse and Lionel Crawford. He said to Naomi, "When we get back to Kentucky, I hope you'll *feng shui* my house the right way." She gave him the come-hither look that he had been hoping for from the first Naomi Barr.

Neutron Star won going away.

DEVIL'S BACKBONE

Intrepid explorers lazily floated down the river on July Fourth in 1799 when an abandoned stone fortress high on the hill of the peninsula jutting out from the north shore came into view. The men drifted on until they could go no further and docked their flatboat near the falls. One of them scouted the area for Indians, but all he found were six skeletons clad in brass breastplates emblazoned with a Welsh coat of arms.

A couple reminiscent of a Quaker deacon and his wife entered Coleman Rare Books on a cool, crisp October morning that signaled the change in seasons. The proprietor introduced himself and asked how he could help as he shelved a crusty, oversized book. They tendered their names in response: Owen and Rotha Gwynedd. The husband nervously shuffled around and fidgeted for a while before getting down to business. "I've got a book here that's been in our family for many years. Can you tell us what it says?"

Felix Coleman snickered to himself, walked over, opened the book carefully, and studied the text for more than a minute. It was an unintelligible left-to-right narrative that he did not recognize. "I'm sorry, sir. I've never seen this language, and I've seen most if not all of them," he replied, handing the book back to the wife without fanfare.

Felix Coleman wasn't the typical dumpy, disheveled bookseller with a rogue hairdo. He was fastidious, sported short-cropped hair, a natural tan, and wore a coat and tie to work every day. He graduated from Bellarmine several years ago with a degree in English and had been peddling rare books out of the same storefront on Louisville's Whiskey Row ever since.

"Is there anyone you know of who could decipher it?" she asked.

"Maybe a cryptologist could for a price. It might take him several weeks."

The wife shifted from one foot to the other and said diffidently, "Would you please send it to one of them for us? We're anxious to know what the book says. We expect to pay."

"I suppose. I can't make any guarantees. Leave it with me for four weeks, and I'll see if anyone can break the code." He smiled at them professionally, though he did not intend to have the text decoded yet.

Felix's operation had not escaped the attention of the police department. Detective Karen Fortier had been trying half-heartedly to catch him selling forgeries and laundering money for years, which he, in fact, had been doing. An anonymous forger sent him a letter twenty years ago detailing a scheme that involved putting books to be duplicated along with cash payments in envelopes and placing them in a locked storage bin at Cuban Hills Cigar Bar. Originals and brilliantly done copies appeared in the bin three weeks later if the offers were accepted.

"We'll come back in a month. Thank you." The wife pushed up the wire-rimmed glasses she was wearing and winced slightly from habit as she followed "the deacon" out the door.

Felix put the peculiar book and some cash in an envelope and stuck a note on the door that read, "Back in fifteen minutes." He proceeded down the street to Cuban Hills, where he placed it in the storage bin.

Owen and Rotha sluggishly pushed open the door of the bookstore again in mid-November and ushered in the essence of a pleasant, Indian-summer afternoon. Felix peered up from his desk with alacrity, waggled his necktie knot, and asked brightly, "How are you folks?"

"We're well, thank you," answered the husband. He appeared more relaxed than on their first visit. "Have you learned anything about our book?"

"The cryptologist said the words are pure gibberish. Unfortunately, they don't say anything. Someone must have whimsically made them up for the fun of it. I'm sorry."

The couple looked at one another in a flash and were visibly disconsolate. The wife spoke. "That's very disappointing." She batted her eyes as if she was preparing to cry.

Felix said, "If you like, I can make you an offer for the book. It is somewhat of a novelty."

"How much are you thinking?"

"Five hundred." The couple seemed stunned. Neither of them said anything. Felix went on, "Look, I'll write a bill of sale and give you a check for that amount. Take them and the book with you. If you decide to sell, just drop it off or mail it to me and then cash the check." He prepared the paperwork with celerity and handed it to them. As they exited, puzzled expressions were plastered on their faces.

The unseasonably cold day before Thanksgiving turned gray, and a few wispy flakes of snow swirled around as cars cut through them on Main Street. Felix began to feel the loneliness of the holiday season, so he closed early and went to Cuban Hills for a smoke and tall Knob Creek single-barrel bourbon on shaved ice. He picked up the *Courier-Journal* and nominally read the headlines when he got there. He did a double take when he leafed through the obituaries.

Owen and Rotha Gwynedd were killed on November 22nd in a fire that consumed their home. There are no records of children or known relatives in the area. Anyone that has any information about the couple or knew them should contact Louisville police. Arson has not been ruled out.

Felix threw down the paper, took a sip of his drink, and rubbed his chin.

Karen Fortier blasted through the swinging doors at the morgue, expecting to get in and out of there in a hurry. She was a pigeon-toed, angular woman of forty-three who gyrated her arms and shoulders when she walked. Her horse face was long and thin, but her comely black hair made it seem proportionally correct. "Well?" she offered as the coroner turned around to face her.

He said, "Nice to see you too, Karen." He delayed giving her the information she came for until she demonstrated proper respect for his craft. "They died of carbon monoxide poisoning. The furnace could have malfunctioned, killing them in their sleep, and then exploded, catching the house on fire."

"That's baloney. Somebody killed 'em and torched the place. They struck me as the kind of people that had a hoard of gold in the house that somebody knew about." Karen scanned the coroner up and down during a moment of silence. She sensed he was bucking for a compliment, which she gave him. "Great work. Let me know if you find anything else."

Karen got in her car and drove east on Interstate 71, exiting at the town of Prospect. Leaves were off the deciduous trees, making them seem moribund, and the dilapidated houses inhabited by river rats were in plain sight now. She worked her way along the Ohio River, away from Louisville, until the burned-out Gwynedd house came into view atop a limestone escarpment to the south of the winding, fissured road. She asked one of the forensic crewman working in the rubble if anything interesting had been found.

He said, "Yes. This fireproof strongbox was in the bedroom closet. I haven't tried to open it yet."

"Here, let me have it. I'll take it downtown." She took the box that was in the plastic bag and carried it off like a loaf of bread.

On the second day of the New Year, Karen Fortier let a frigid, biting breeze waft into Coleman Rare Books on purpose, just to aggravate Felix Coleman, who was sitting placidly at his tidy desk along the wall. He stood up and said, "Karen. Good to see you again. You've decided to take me up on my offer for dinner and a night at the opera?"

"I'd consider it if you weren't such a scoundrel." The strongbox was dangling from her right hand. Karen continued, "So, I take it the Gwynedds came in your shop last fall. I see where you tried to buy this." She opened the box to show him the book, bill of sale, and uncashed check.

"I did."

"Nice try. I had this book carbon and protein dated. It's only two months old. That means you copied the original and fobbed this fake off on them. I want the real thing back. It belongs to their estate." She closed the lid of the strongbox with a clap and snap.

"I deal in so many books, I don't really remember what happened two months ago." Felix sat down again and feigned busywork.

Karen leaned on his desk and propped herself on her left arm before saying, "Okay, if you want to play it that way, I understand. I'm going to hang you out to dry on this one." She grabbed all of the pens and pencils in the holder on his desk and took them with her, just to needle him again.

Felix received a letter in the mail the following Monday that had red and blue diagonal stripes around the border, similar to an old airmail envelope. He flattened the creases in the enclosed typewritten vellum and read what it said:

Felix,

I want to buy the Gwynedd manuscript from you. Meet me at Taberna el Norte at noon tomorrow. I'll be wearing a red sweater. Bring the book. I'll pay you one million dollars in un-marked bills on the spot. Otherwise, I'll send evidence to the police of your book forging business.

He tucked the letter back in the envelope and put it in the locked drawer of his desk. Felix received the exact same letter three days in a row. The final demand came on the fourth day. He had one more chance before the police would be notified.

Felix closed the shop, threw the envelope with the book in it on the passenger seat of his car, and drove cautiously down Bardstown Road. He parked behind Taberna el Norte in a grease-covered, asphalt lot that needed to be repaved. The inviting aroma of the restaurant was negated by the sticky smell of rancid cooking oil that had been overused. When he stepped through the back door, he spotted the man in the red sweater. The man turned in his direction and smiled. Just then, Felix felt two men hook his arms on either side. The one on the left said, "We're the police. Come with us."

"I'm not sure what you did is legal. I'd call it entrapment." The interrogation room at the police station was a putrid shade darker than a pleasant yellow. Felix dropped his head, wove his hands, and set them on the galvanized sheet-metal table.

Karen replied, "Let's make a deal. You give me the book, and I'll lay off your shady business for a while. I might even throw in that dinner and a night at the opera you've been hounding me about."

"Deal." Felix stood up and paraded out of the room with aplomb.

The second of February was one of those days that teased people into believing that winters in Kentucky weren't that bad. Karen Fortier took her time sauntering over to Coleman Rare Books to enjoy the fair weather. She closed the front door after stepping through it and said, "Felix, just when I start to warm up to you a little bit, wham, you double-cross me again. Why do you do that?"

"What now?" He felt something bad was on the horizon.

"I had the book you gave me dated the same way I did the other copy, and guess what? It's only three months old. So, what the hell is going on?"

"I'll help you, Karen, but you'll have to cut me some slack," he said aimlessly. Felix explained in great detail the process he used to get books duplicated. He surmised, "I suppose the forger made two or three copies. The bona fide book must be worth something. Did you happen to find a cryptologist that could interpret it?"

"They're working on it," she answered. "Look, let's put something in the bin at Cuban Hills and see who the pickup man is."

"I'm pretty sure it's the bartender. Follow him when he leaves work to see where he drops it off."

The bartender pulled away from Cuban Hills at 10:20 that evening with the police trailing at a distance. He drove west and then south on 264 to the Bells Lane exit. The neighborhood had its share of falling-down commercial buildings awaiting demolition. He stopped at a ramshackle house, got out, and pushed the envelope through a mail slot in the front door.

Karen Fortier paid another visit to Coleman Rare Books the next afternoon. Cold sunshine washed the books with a warm light that heightened the musty smell of the arcane tomes stacked there. Felix Coleman came from the back of the store to meet her. "Well, what did you find out?"

"The bartender dropped the package off at the home of Aksel and Gisla Royse. From what I've been able to find out, she's a cryptologist, and he's an artist. I suspect he's the forger. Here are pictures of them from their drivers' licenses."

Felix studied the photos, and a disgusted expression instantly contorted his face. "I've seen these people before. That's the couple that came in here with the book and told me they were Owen and Rotha Gwynedd."

"They brought you a fake? What the hell were they trying to do?"

"My guess is the real Gwynedds took the original to them to be deciphered. Gisla must have figured out what the book said and thought it was valuable, which meant she asked Aksel to make several copies while she kept the genuine article. I bet they told Owen and Rotha they couldn't decipher the language and sent them on their way with a duplicate."

Karen asked, "Then why come in here and try to pull a con?"

"You want the criminal version?" Felix stared into her eyes. He began to think that he could get out of this mess yet. "They planned on keeping the original, killing those people and implicating me for the murder. They were expecting me to run the normal forgery scam on them and sell what I thought was the original to an anonymous European buyer. They must have gassed the Gwynedds and put their forged copy of the book and the paperwork I gave Royse in the fireproof strongbox before setting the place on fire. What they didn't count on was me falling for your blackmail trap."

"I think I'll go visit these shysters and innocently try to find out if Owen and Rotha brought them any business," Karen announced.

"I'd be careful. By the way, were you able to get the text decoded?"

She grinned and said, "Yeah. It's some phonic form of a twelfth-century Welsh language, a one-off. People from Wales were illiterate then, but there must have been one oddball who was smart enough to chronicle the events of the times."

"What's the story about?" Felix quizzed.

"It's the tale of a guy by the name of Madoc Gwynedd who sailed to America from Wales in eleven seventy. He and his party rowed up to the Falls of the Ohio River, where they ran into Indian trouble. The Falls was the central trading place for various tribes at that time. Madoc went a little further up the river and found a peninsula he could colonize to protect his clan from invasion. Today they call it Devil's Backbone.

Felix spouted, "Do you know what that means? If the original book actually dates back to the twelfth century, it's worth a bloody fortune. I hope you can get your hands on it."

"I'll let you know what happens. When this is over, you'd better get those opera tickets, and dinner reservations lined up," she commanded with a hint of flirtation.

Karen Fortier hadn't been seen in three days, and everybody on the police force began to wonder if something bad had happened to her. After three weeks, she officially became a missing person.

The window washer took his articulated squeegee on April Fools' Day and deftly swiped the front windows of Coleman Rare Books to remove the grime that had built up over the winter. Felix stepped out front and handed him a twenty-dollar bill. When he looked down the sidewalk, far off, there came Aksel and Gisla Royse. He stepped back inside, called the police, and quickly unlocked the top drawer of his desk. The couple entered the shop and no longer displayed the naive countenance they aped on their first two visits. "What did you do with the copy of the last book I did for you?"

"Why, shucks, Mister Gwynedd, what big teeth you have. Has your wife gone rabid too?"

"Cut the crap. I want the book back."

"Is that so? After all the trouble you've caused me?"

"You mean twenty years of making forgeries for you counts for nothing? You owe me." Aksel looked as restless as a caged cougar.

Felix yanked open the desk drawer and pulled out the pistol. "I gave it to the police. Now get out of here, and don't come back." Aksel immediately lurched over the desk and wrenched the gun out of Felix's hand. They wrestled wildly on the floor until the front door swung open with a vengeance.

A policeman stepped in and hollered, "Hold it! I'll take that."

Aksel stood up, shrugged his shoulders, straightened his outfit, and said, "He drew a gun on me." Felix rotated his neck and jaw and said nothing. He picked up the firearm and surrendered it.

"It's all over now." The policeman roughly ushered the Royse couple out and instructed them to go home. When the cop returned to the bookstore, he had a package with him. "We found this on Karen's desk. It's addressed to you. Since we don't know if we'll ever see her again, I thought you should open it in case it has any clues as to her whereabouts."

Felix ripped it open to find *The Tale of Madoc Gwynedd*. The note in the inside cover read:

Felix,

I used a search warrant to get into the Royse house. There were two books there, but I'm sure this is the original. Don't tell anybody that you got it from me. The court cashed your check and signed the bill of sale, so the book is legally yours. It should more than pay for that dinner and night at the opera.

Karen

Felix Coleman gazed through the newly cleaned shop windows and saw visions of sugarplums. Soon, he would be rich.

On July Fourth, the Ohio River was a deep green and relatively low for that time of year. A body was found in the woods on Devil's Backbone by a hiker who had strayed where he didn't belong. The remains, covered in ancient Welsh armor, were those of Detective Karen Fortier.

WHO IS THAT LADY?

Leo Palmer had been working at Ruby Hollow Horse Farm in Ocala for fourteen years when Mark Ruby let him know that the operation had been sold. It wasn't a surprise since, as the accountant, he had prepared countless financial schedules over the last year that portended such an event. The farm just wasn't making enough money to hold Mark's interest. He certainly would have enjoyed it more if Leo hadn't been embezzling a little over $100K a year. Leo worked a kickback scheme with a supplier the first year he started at the farm. Everything happened in cash, which meant his personal safe got loaded to the gills with stacks of stolen hundreds amassed over years of exemplary service for Ruby.

Leo lived under a lucky star. He applied for an accountant's job at Pin Fire Stud in Paris, Kentucky, that had just been bought by a bigger-than-life Scotsman. Hamish Iverach's people called Mark Ruby for a reference on Leo when his resume came in. They hired him sight unseen. Leo loaded his packed safe and what little else he owned in a moving van bound for the tiny guest house at the back of the Pin Fire property, and then took a plane to Las Vegas for two days of fun before settling into his new job.

Hamish Iverach had lived in Scotland his whole life. His business in Inverness, Teach Them Young, was world renowned. Rich people sent their children to his "training centers" to learn how to be leaders, innovators, and entrepreneurs. The first curriculum for six-year-olds was "Profitable Hobbies." Next came "Impressing People" at age eight. By ten, the little tykes were taught about

"Seizing Opportunities." Twelve-year-olds got a full dose of "A Value Proposition." The crown jewel of the indoctrination, "Entrepreneurial Mentality," attracted wealthy fourteen-year-olds from democracies and dictatorships alike.

The last two offerings from Teach Them Young were for mid-to-late teens, "Emotional IQ" and "Financial Savvy." The staff had an unwritten "matchmaking" program for those ages that parents endorsed when they wanted their kids to find a rich mate to plus-up the family wealth. Hamish had also boiled the entire curricula down to a "traveling show" that dozens of instructors took on the road. Profits skyrocketed and kept on flowing into the coffers. At that point, Hamish Iverach retired from the business and partied nonstop, so much so that his Scottish neighbors considered him a disturbance and nuisance. He obliged them by selling.

Pin Fire Stud came into being through a combination of a mansion carved off an adjoining farm that couldn't afford to keep it up, and a working farm to the north that had some of the best pasture and barns in the business. Iverach dumped millions of dollars in the place, adding a party pavilion and chef's kitchen. Soon it became a popular venue for social events. The noise and the traffic in the area sent the neighbors into apoplexy. The donations to charities sent the community into euphoria. The hot ticket now, sort of a status symbol, was to be invited to one of the farm's high-profile parties.

The palpable energy and ephemera at a Pin Fire Stud fundraising event tended to open wallets wider than usual. Piper Lee grabbed a smoked-salmon canapé to go with her watered-down Wild Turkey when the waiter waded through the crowd with a platter. She saw a woman that could be her identical twin heading in her direction. "Hey, am I imagining things, or do we kind of look alike?" said Jade Richardson. "What a great get-together!" A pianist played familiar songs in the background accompanied by an electric violin. A gusty breeze took the edge off the intense, late-day sunshine. There were hundreds of black, white, and silver German luxury cars parked in the field behind the party barn.

"I like your hairdo better. Piper Lee." She presented her hand on a foreshortened arm.

Jade did a quick chop of a handshake, responded with her own name, and then asked, "How'd you get invited to this bash?"

"Oh, I have a legal filing business. I handle names and bloodstock registrations for many of the horse farms, liens and titles for a lot of car dealers, copyrights and trademarks for writers, and compliance paperwork for stockbrokers and a few distilleries in the area. I'm cheaper than attorneys. What about you?"

Jade said, "I just moved here from Texas. I sell betting information to horseplayers at Gulfstream, Churchill Downs, Keeneland, Santa Anita, Saratoga, and Oaklawn. There's less cheating at those tracks."

"How does that work?" Piper expressed sincere interest in the vocation.

"I spent five years programming algorithms that evaluate the outcomes of horse races. I took thousands of data sets of track condition, number of horses in a race, postposition, and odds for each horse three minutes before the race, and compared it to the actual race results. What it told me was how to bet a race for the highest probability of cashing a ticket."

"Does it work?"

Jade looked indignant. "Well, of course. I enter the data in my programs three minutes before post time, get the betting strategy, and then send a text blast to my subscribers no later than two minutes before post time. Some races are inconclusive, so I take a pass on them."

"Do you do that every day?" Piper asked.

"Heavens no. I work noon to eight Tuesday through Friday. No weekend races. I only support professional handicappers that want to win money quietly during the week. Plus, I don't want to drag down weekend pools and call attention to my system."

"Fascinating. So, if I bet like you say to every race you call in a year, what would my return be?"

Jade sniggered and averted Piper's eyes. "Thirty-seven percent. But there is a catch. The higher the amount bet, the lower the return due to pool percentages."

Piper contemplated that and replied, "Which means you have to limit the subscriptions, right?"

"Exactly. I keep two hundred subscribers that pay me two thousand a year. I've been doing this for six years now, and nearly all of my players are repeat customers. One of them got me invited to this affair. Part of the sales pitch is the limited amount of subscriptions. I also personally bet the races that have very high probabilities. The annual return on those is around sixty percent."

"I'll be damned." Piper's wheels were turning. "Since both of us have stay-at-home businesses, would you be interested in getting a place together? Living alone can be a drag sometimes."

"Yes, I would." Jade moved off to commandeer a tiny tenderloin sandwich. She returned, handed Piper a business card, and said, "Call me."

Hamish Iverach, in an exuberant mood, sat on the veranda of his mansion, sipping coffee beside the new accountant. "Leo, what were the donations yesterday?"

"Two hundred seventy-three thousand dollars. The goal was a quarter of a million," he replied.

"Good. Everybody should be pleased. You know, I've been thinking about a new business venture." Iverach walked over to the wrought-iron porch railing. He sniffed the pungent smell of cut grass.

"What's that, sir?"

"It's called 'Raise Them Right.' I've done a lot of research over the years on how to raise children for success. I want to put together a curriculum that helps them achieve it." He turned away from the railing and set his coffee cup on the table. "The crux of it is to be a generalist."

"Come again, sir?" He wanted to keep the conversation going.

"It would take all morning to explain it. Here is an example. Who becomes the better musician, the child that is forced to practice violin eight hours a day starting at age ten, or the kid that knocks around on several instruments before settling on one by age twenty? Children shouldn't be raised as prodigies." Iverach looked at Palmer to see if he halfway understood the idea.

"What about Tiger Woods?"

Hamish blustered, "He was definitely a prodigy, but just think if he would have played football, basketball, and soccer growing up, how much better at golf he would be. Look at Roger Federer. He dabbled in skiing, wrestling, skateboarding, squash, handball, basketball, ping-pong, and soccer. He didn't specialize in tennis until he had trained his body as a versatile athlete."

"Point taken."

"This idea of being a generalist isn't just about athletics. It's more about the mind than the body. One thing I've noticed about people in the United States, they no longer value an intellect unless the kid is a total klutz. Then he's relegated to intellectual things. The whole concept of my program is to develop the physical, mental, emotional, and spiritual side of a person in balance, a Renaissance man, knowledgeable and proficient in a wide range of fields. That is the best preparation for success in life."

The accountant wanted to know where all this was going. "I get it now. Anything I can do to help?"

"Yes, Leo. Find me someone that can manipulate databases and develop algorithms. This whole thing comes down to time management. What are all the things children should be doing with their time from age four to age eighteen, and when should they be doing it? That's a curriculum I can sell, and it has to have solid research behind it." Iverach heard his cell phone ringing in the kitchen and went to retrieve it.

Piper Lee and Jade Richardson found a 150-year-old house to rent on the Kentucky River that had been beautifully redone. The stone alcazar was immured by limestone Palisades that gave it a claustrophobic feel, yet one of being exceptionally secure. The boat dock on the river had graceful, flowing trees hovering overhead that offered satisfying shade on hot days. Jade spent a small fortune on the best computer systems and communication equipment available, so she could operate from there at a high level.

"Why don't you have a guy?" Jade asked.

Piper wagged her head and glanced to the right. "I guess because I'm technically still married."

"Huh?"

"Travis Lee. He didn't come home one night. I hired detectives. So did his parents. No trace."

"Well, that's a hell of a thing."

"What about you?" Piper reciprocated.

"I'm really picky. Smart men are generally wimps, and manly men are usually not very smart. Looking for Mister Right, I guess." Jade's cell phone rang. "Hello."

"This is Leo Palmer over at Pin Fire Stud."

"Yes?" Jade knew what he would say next.

"I got your name from someone that uses your services," Leo stated.

"I'm sorry, sir. I only sell a limited amount of subscriptions. I fill all of them between Christmas and New Year's for the following season. If you'll call back then, I'll know if one is available."

"I'm afraid you misunderstand me. You came recommended as one of the best data analysts and algorithm writers in the country. Mister Hamish Iverach, who owns the farm here, would like to hire you for a special project."

Jade switched gears in her mind and responded, "I really don't have the time."

Leo interrupted her to say, "Three hundred dollars an hour, and it will likely take a year."

Jade did the math in her head. "When can I come by and chat with you about it?"

"Whatever fits your schedule?"

Leo Palmer did a double take when he first saw Jade Richardson march into the room two days later with her hand projected out, offering to shake. They made small talk until Hamish joined them. Pleasantries were exchanged, and then Hamish talked for nearly two hours. He was a manly man and smart as a whip, but too old for her. Leo was the right age, but she hadn't quite figured him out yet. He was good-looking enough. When she left, her mind churned everything she had heard. Piper would have to help out to make the deal go.

The first six months were the hardest because of the monotony of gathering the data. Eleven months into the project, the work was finally complete. Jade had trained Piper to run the handicapping business and manipulate the data in Iverach's brainchild. The curricula would be purchased online. The menu allowed for some flexibility, like choosing which vegetable to have with an entree. Jade knew that the program she had meticulously developed would be worth twenty times the half million-plus that he had paid for it. Piper, with Jade's constant coaching, put the finishing touches on an impressive PowerPoint for Raise Them Right. It had screenshots and interactive links to the real thing, and was ready to be presented.

Jade slapped the tops of her thighs with both hands and beckoned, "Let's go out on the dock to celebrate and watch the boats go by. Get the champagne I bought and two glasses." They had been sitting, chatting, and waving at boaters for nearly an hour when the doorbell rang.

"I'll get it," Piper said. She jumped up, went through the back door, and looked out the front window to see a periwinkle Bentley sports car with a burnt-orange interior and the top down.

She opened the door, stiffened, and said in a squeaky voice, "Travis?"

"Piper?" She fainted. He got back in his car and drove off.

"Who is it, Piper?" When Jade got no response, she went in to find her passed out on the floor and the front door open. Once Piper came to, she explained to Jade what had happened.

"Let's get in my car and chase after him. Come on!" They made a calculated guess that he would be going into Lexington. Jade drove like a maniac over to Harrodsburg Road. She passed every car in her way, even on double-yellow lines. "Are you sure it was him?"

"Yes, he said my name."

"That rat bastard. How long has it been since he disappeared?"

"Fifteen years," Piper replied despondently.

"Do you still love him?"

"Hell no. I want to kill him."

"Let's see if we can corner the bugger." As Harrodsburg Road widened to four lanes, Piper spotted the Bentley nearly a half mile ahead. They lost sight of it several times, but kept going straight, eventually through town and onto Paris Pike. When the car came into view again, it sped up. Just as Jade began to close the distance, the periwinkle juggernaut wheeled into the entrance lane of Pin Fire Stud. The driver swiped a card in the reader, the massive gate opened, and he shot through it. The gate had completely closed by the time Jade skidded up to it. "Well, at least we know where to find him." She looked over her shoulder, backed out onto Paris Pike, and started the trip home. "I've got an idea," she said.

The large TV screen in the conference room at the Pin Fire mansion read "Raise Them Right," announcing the PowerPoint that would be used to kick off Iverach's dream. Leo Palmer sat silently across the table. Hamish spoke with excitement. "Jade, there is something different about you today. I can't put my finger on it."

"It's the look of a happy person that has just finished a year-long project," she said, smiling. For the next hour and forty-five minutes, the three people in the conference room went through the program in great detail. The curricula would be sold online at $999 for each year or $11,999 for all fifteen years, ages four to eighteen. Each sale would have a unique code and copyright warning to guard against piracy. Hard copies of collateral material would also be available for purchase online at various prices. "What do you think?"

Iverach replied, "It's fantastic, just what I envisioned." He looked at Palmer, asking, "Would you leave us for a minute?" Leo got up and exited quietly. "Jade, I know I'm a little old for you, but I would like to escort you to dinner sometime. Would you be interested?"

"Why, yes," she pronounced like an experienced coquette. Hamish nodded to her and scurried out of the conference room, very pleased. While she was packing up the electronics, Leo returned, his face frozen in a rictus grin. She turned to look at him. "Travis, you're still married to Piper Lee, and the wife you once knew isn't around anymore. I still don't understand why you walked out on me. I'm Jade Richardson now, and if you know what's good for you, you'll keep that to yourself."

Leo gave Pin Fire Stud his two-week notice. During that time, he sold the Bentley, bought a new car under the name Travis Lee, and loaded duffle bags of cash in the trunk. He disposed of everything else he owned except his real birth certificate and the clothes on his back. He drove through the night to reach Dallas by the next morning. Jade Richardson, now Piper Lee, had done much the same. When they met up in Texas, Travis said, "I'll follow you to the junkyard." When they got there, Travis gave the man $2,000 and instructed him to crush Jade's car into a cube and bury it at the back of a remote ranch where no one could ever find it.

Hamish Iverach was holding court at the annual fundraiser that he had become famous for. Behind him, four chefs in whites were pressing the grease out of hamburgers and butterflied Italian sausages. The savory aroma occasionally distracted the carefree crowd. "Folks, I want to introduce someone to you. This is Jade Richardson, the person that made Raise Them Right a reality. She is not only beautiful but very smart. We are planning to marry soon. Now, that'll be a *real* party." He peered at her and raised his glass of bourbon. The new Jade Richardson beamed, and he did the same. The people around them groveled like the sycophants they were.

Hamish died seventeen months later. He left everything to Jade. The estate got settled in less than a year. Shortly thereafter, a man by the name of Travis Lee went into court and claimed that the woman posing as Jade Iverach was actually his wife, Piper Lee, and he could prove it. He wanted a divorce and half of her estate. Travis also said the real Jade Richardson had gone missing over two years ago, buried at the back of a Texas ranch somewhere perhaps?

THE DEGAS AT THE DEL RIO

"Asher, what can I get you?" inquired Calvin Burke.

"A Henry Clay Hawk and Colonel Taylor will be fine." Asher Vargas wandered into the Del Rio at about 5:15 most days for a short, mild cigar and tall, stout bourbon with one big ice cube in it. He left by six o'clock unless something unusual distracted him. He was suspicious of everything and everybody. As a detective for the city police department, he knew that things weren't always what they seemed.

"Here you go." Calvin set both items on the burl table that Vargas frequently used as his base camp.

The Del Rio Cigar and Bourbon Bar had changed the pace of life in downtown Frankfort since going into the gentrified storefront a year ago. Calvin Burke and his wife Ginevra took the corner section of the hundred-year-old building and built in a long stainless-steel bar and small food-prep area behind the humidor. The separate room on the backside of the bar had been equipped with TVs, worn-out leather chairs, ashtrays, and industrial-strength air filters. Ginevra's sister, Arianna D'Arcangelo, took the rest of the walled-up space to the left of the bar to fit out an art gallery dedicated to horse racing and scenes of Kentucky.

Their business model for making money was simple—snare as much of the Kentucky Bourbon Trail and Keeneland traffic as possible. The men could smoke, drink, and run their mouths while the women fought off boredom going through the gallery.

If a woman showed much interest in one of the pieces, her man would step up, flaunt his chivalry, and make the purchase for her.

Ginevra and Arianna were children of old-fashioned Italian immigrants. Arianna was younger, smarter, and better looking, but Ginevra had a warm persona that transcended all those other things. That's why she had a man and Arianna didn't. The artwork in the gallery ran to a much higher level than what a run-of-the-mill Kentuckian could afford or appreciate. It fit Arianna's high-brow personality. She had built impressive contacts among equine and nature artists by virtue of her good looks. She knew very well that many of the Bourbon Trail trekkers were gentry from big cities, and most of the pieces needed to capture their romantic vision of the Bluegrass.

And then there was the painting for sale that Arianna didn't remember seeing, buying or hanging, yet there it was, priced at $25,000. A couple walked up, and the man asked, "Is that a real Degas?" The picture depicted a rear view of racehorses with jockeys atop, in different colored silks, approaching the starting line. The spired grandstands were shadowed in on the left.

Arianna assessed the couple's likelihood of being able to shell out the price before answering, "I doubt it. I'm sure it's a copy."

"I don't know," the man said. He scrunched his face and looked closely at the lower right-hand corner of the painting. "That's a very authentic-looking signature."

Arianna replied soothingly, "Well, I'm representing it as a copy."

"Would you mind if we looked at the back?" Arianna unhooked the piece from the wall and flipped it over for the couple to inspect. "The canvas sure looks a hundred and fifty years old."

The woman tapped the bottom corner of the frame and said, "Look here. It says the Etta Cone Collection. Who's that?"

"She and her sister were famous art collectors from Baltimore, my dear." The man looked up and studied the burnt-umber, tin ceiling tiles for a few seconds. He had made up his mind. "We'll take the painting. Whether it's real or not, we can certainly impress our friends with it." He reached in his coat pocket for the checkbook.

Arianna was careful to write "reproduction" on the invoice to avoid being accused of selling a fake for the real thing. After concluding the sale, she began frantically going through purchase records to see if she had ever bought such a work of art. Nothing came up.

Black, low-scudding clouds laden with rain cast a dark blanket over the windows of the Del Rio. Asher Vargas took his regular seat away from the front door of the bar and noticed that he was the only customer in the house. Sprinkles of rain began to splatter on the window. "Calvin, I want to try a Mombacho and Wild Turkey Rare Breed."

"We sold an Edgar Degas copy this afternoon for twenty-five thousand," Calvin barked as he plopped a big cube in a tall glass.

"Good for you. Does that mean you can cut the prices on cigars and drinks?"

"No, raise them to get rid of the riffraff."

"I'm the only person in here. It looks like to me you could use some more riffraff. Oh, I get it. I'm the riffraff you want to get rid of." Vargas rarely displayed such a sense of humor.

"You're not married, are you, Asher?" Calvin delivered the drink and cigar.

"No."

"Ever consider asking my sister-in-law out? She's quite a looker."

Vargas shifted his eyes to the side and rested his front teeth on his thumb. "No."

"Better move in before somebody else does."

Several days later, Arianna went to the freight dock at the back of the gallery and noticed a crate without a label. Inside was a Degas that looked like the one she had sold to the couple that recently came through. She began to worry that they were returning the painting for a refund. On the back of the piece, she saw the inscription that read, "Clairibel Cone Collection."

Arianna tracked Ginevra down to get her attention. "Ginny, something weird is going on."

"What?" She studied her sister's face, reading her disposition.

"I sold a painting a few days ago for twenty-five thousand that I have no record of ever buying, and now another one just like it is out back. What should I do?"

"Sell it too, I reckon. The artist will turn up eventually to get paid. Don't worry about it." Ginevra had often bolstered Arianna's courage in times of doubt.

"Thing is, these fakes are incredibly good. I could probably sell one a week for the next ten years."

Ginevra replied, "So, when the artist does come around, try to keep them coming."

It took less than a week for the same scenario as last time to play out.

Calvin filled Vargas in on the sale of the second painting. He responded, "I don't like it. A forger is using this gallery to pedal the same work of art. Wonder how many copies there are? Worse yet, I wonder if someone plans to extort Arianna after the fact. Keep me informed. This could end up as police business."

The Del Rio only sold Kentucky-made bourbons that were commercially available. The shelves were arranged by distillery to align with stops on the Bourbon Trail. Cigars were a different story.

Vendors kept trying to muscle their sought-after brands into the limited humidor space at the expense of more obscure titles, and if Vargas wanted a particular smoke, Calvin stocked it for obvious reasons. "Asher, you need to try one of these Nicaraguan Quattro's. They are the highest-ranked robustos in the world." He waved one at him from behind the bar. "By the way, can you explain how this art saga might become police business?" he probed.

"If several forgeries of the same painting are so good that one or more are deemed authentic, then somebody in law enforcement will want to know what is going on. The science of spotting forgeries has gotten sophisticated, yet plenty of fakes still get through."

Calvin began to feel uneasy as he uttered woodenly, "I see."

The next day at two thirty in the afternoon, Arianna was stricken with dread when she saw the unmarked crate on the shipping dock. She removed another Degas copy and looked on the back of the canvas to find "Gertrude Stein Collection" in faded ink. An envelope had been taped along the top edge of the canvas. Inside was an invoice, key card for a hotel room, and letter that read:

Arianna D'Arcangelo,

Enclosed is an invoice for three Degas reproductions in the amount of $30,000. Please make the check out to Ginevra Burke and record payment in full for the three artworks in the note section. That will provide you with proof of payment. Have Ginevra cash the check and the cash brought to Room 451 in the Benchmark Hotel (key enclosed) at ten o'clock tomorrow morning. Instruct whoever delivers the cash to leave the envelope of money on the bed and throw away the key after leaving. If I don't get the money, Ginevra will be accused as the forger. We don't want that.

Calvin Burke

Arianna handed Calvin the letter, and he questioned rhetorically, "What kind of scam is this? Why did this bum use my name?" He ceremoniously dropped the letter on the bar and appeared completely dismayed. "I need to show this to Asher."

Vargas came through the door at the usual time, and Burke accosted him on the spot. "I want you to look at something." He handed him the letter. Vargas read it, did an about-face, and left without a word.

The Benchmark overlooked a bend in the Kentucky River. It was classified as a boutique hotel and had four floors of rooms that were uniquely decorated. The marble in the lobby gave guests a sense of being back in time. The price to stay there didn't. "Miss, I'm from the police department." Vargas flashed his badge. "Did you check someone into room four-fifty-one earlier today?"

The middle-aged woman was seventy pounds overweight and wore too much makeup. "Yes, I did." She tapped the computer and stated, "Calvin Burke is his name."

"What did he look like?"

"He was about your height, had a long black beard, black hat, and wore some sort of tunic, toga or cassock, or whatever you call it."

"Like an Orthodox Jew?"

The woman batted her eyes and replied, "Yes, that's it. He asked for four-fifty-one, which was empty, so I gave it to him. He showed me his passport, wanted two keys, paid cash, and walked back out that door." She pointed straight ahead.

"Didn't go up the elevator?"

"No."

"Do you have a security camera that might have his picture on it?"

"We don't have any cameras in the hotel, sir."

"Is four-fifty-two across the hall vacant? I would like to rent it."

"It is. How do you want to pay for it?"

Vargas reached in his wallet for a credit card. "I need to look inside four-fifty-one if you don't mind."

"I'll have the bellman let you in."

Vargas stopped for a sandwich and decaf coffee on the way back to the Del Rio. The clock on the back wall read 6:33 when he entered the bar again. The place was loud and loaded with people.

"Calvin, let me try that Quattro you were talking about, and put about an inch of Maker's forty-six in a tall glass and the rest water."

"What happened to you? Where'd you go?"

"I went over to the Benchmark Hotel to see if I could catch whoever did this." He pulled the letter out and gave it back. "My guess is the person used a disguise to check into the hotel and is here right now watching what's going on. I want to take a close look at everybody, and then set a trap for the culprit tomorrow."

"What do you think about the demand?" Calvin asked.

"I like it. It gives Arianna a chance to pay for the forgeries and get a proof of purchase, and gives me a chance to catch a forger."

"How do you want to play it?"

"Have your wife and Arianna meet me here at eight thirty in the morning." He made a show of scrutinizing each of the patrons in the house until closing time.

Vargas looked through the window of the Del Rio the next morning to see if the sisters were there. A loud leaf blower distracted him momentarily. The door of the bar opened slowly to reveal Arianna's beautiful face. She put forth a disheartened smile. "Come now, Arianna, why the sad expression?"

"This business has me in knots," she said.

"Well, it shouldn't. You've made some good money selling paintings lately. Today, we'll clean this thing up, so brighten that pretty face of yours."

"Easy for you to say. You're used to dealing with murderers, thieves, and drug dealers. Not me."

Ginevra walked up and greeted Vargas. He said to her, "Let's go over the plan. Where's Calvin?"

"He has his routine. Goes to the gym first thing. Then he fixes a big brunch for himself before coming to work at eleven. He said if we need him to call."

Vargas thought to himself, if only Arianna had Ginevra's personality, she would be the catch of the century. He was starting to think she was a damn good catch anyway. "All right. Arianna, make a check out to Ginevra like the letter stated. Then call the bank and let them know that your sister will be over to cash it. I presume you are in favor of paying for the paintings?"

"Yes."

"Good. At ten o'clock, let's all go over to the Benchmark and put the cash on the bed in four-fifty-one. Be sure to bring the room key."

"I guess I better take an envelope over to the bank big enough to hold thirty thousand," Ginevra commented.

"After you guys leave the hotel, I'll rig up the door on four-fifty-one to buzz me when it gets opened. I'll be across the hall in four-fifty-two. Then I can jump over and catch somebody red-handed."

At a little before ten o'clock, the three of them met in the lobby of the Benchmark, and proceeded to the fourth floor. Arianna swiped the key card on the latch of the room until the green light appeared. Ginevra threw the envelope of cash onto the middle of the bed as Vargas went through the place carefully. He remarked, "Nobody's been here yet. You can head out. Arianna, I'll get rid of that door key for you." The sisters went into the hall and stopped to watch Vargas stick electrical contacts on the door edge. He let the door shut and waved to them as he stepped into the room across the hall.

They returned to the Del Rio and waited for Calvin to arrive at work. When he came in soon after eleven o'clock, he asked, "Did everything go as planned?"

"It did. Now we'll find out who's pulling this stunt," said Arianna.

The Del Rio got slammed late in the afternoon by a tour bus full of raconteurs and blowhards that had just come from Buffalo Trace Distillery. Arianna ran around the gallery answering questions while Calvin and Ginevra doled out drinks and appetizers as fast as they could. People that traveled on busses generally drank a snoot full, and this group didn't disappoint.

Vargas came into the bar at four thirty, face sagging. He went over to Calvin Burke and said quietly, "Get me a Punch cigar. I can't have anything to drink until after five."

"What happened, Asher?"

"I waited across the hall for several hours, and nobody came. I got antsy and checked to make sure the money was still there. Gone. I looked around and saw that one of the ceiling tiles in the bathroom had been dislodged. I got the maintenance man to bring up a ladder. It looks like someone knew how to climb around in the attic to get in and back out of the room."

"That sounds fishy to me."

Vargas fired back, "I'll tell you what's fishy. You using your own name on the letter and hotel reservation. The Orthodox Jew getup was a nice touch."

"What are you talking about?" Calvin backed away from him as though he were radioactive.

"Come on, Calvin, you're the one that stole the money. Running short on cash, are you? I knew it was going to be you when you didn't show up this morning. A little too obvious, don't you think?"

"Ah, but you're overlooking one thing. I have an ironclad alibi. I was at my accountant's office from eight until eleven this morning. A half dozen people saw me there, and two of them walked with me over here when I left." Calvin moved to within a foot of Asher's face. "Want to take back what you said?"

"Can't blame me for trying. If you had done it, I wanted you to confess. No hard feelings?"

"Hey, how can I have hard feelings toward the guy that helped my sister-in-law make a lot of money selling paintings?"

"What do you mean?" Vargas went on the defensive.

"What's bothered me all along is why you took a sleepy detective job in Frankfort. I checked out your background. You worked in Baltimore and your claim to fame is catching one of the most notorious forgers in the world known for doing the same work of art over and over. You got those horse forgeries from him and came here to sell them discreetly. It must have been really easy just to walk across the hall at the hotel and pocket the thirty thousand. As you said, the Orthodox Jew getup was a nice touch. You planned to blame it on me to see if I had an alibi or not. I can't prove any of this, and don't really care to." Calvin stared blankly at Vargas and asked, "Want that drink now?"

Another unmarked crate stood perched on the gallery loading dock a week later. Arianna opened it to find a fourth Degas, only this one was different from the other three. It had no Degas signature on the canvas, but did have a "Certificate of Authenticity" from a highly respected art appraisal company.

Vargas came in the Del Rio at 5:20 that afternoon. Arianna went over and told him what had appeared behind the shop earlier that day. He said, "Everybody knows that Degas didn't sign a lot of his artwork. I bet its worth a million dollars." Her eyes got big and a Mona Lisa grin formed on her face. He suggested, "You're loaded. Why don't we go to Jeff Ruby's over in Lexington to celebrate?"

"I'd like that," Arianna said as she touched Vargas on the shoulder.

You Can't Ski While Reciting Poetry

Clark Buxton parked behind his storefront business in downtown Paducah at 8:50 a.m. on a sweltering morning that presaged a scorching-hot day. The weary mood that had dogged him the last several weeks persisted. He hadn't made any real money since flipping a big purchase over a year ago, and was selling off his own set of Morgan silver dollars to pay the bills. Coin collecting was inexorably dying. There wasn't even enough margin in bullion to eke out a decent living anymore.

Everything was on the internet now. Shops were closing like all bricks and mortar. Clark kept on hoping someone would walk in with a $100,000 collection that he could cadge for half its value, or a spinster would call who wanted to sell her hoard for next to nothing. His phone began to bleat as he keyed open the brass lock on the back door of the shop. He answered with, "Blackthorn Gold and Coin. How can I help you?"

"This is Martin Cox. Do you guys do appraisals?"

"Yes. Bring in what you've got, and I'll put a price on it."

Cox hesitated before saying, "Well, that's not so easy. The stuff I have is in big plastic tubs. There must be two hundred pounds here. Any way you could come out and look at it? I live in Bardwell. I'm thinking the whole thing is worth maybe a half million."

"Sure. We charge one hundred dollars an hour for an appraisal unless we buy the collection. I'd be happy to take a look at it."

"When can I expect you?"

"Give me your address and I'll run by this afternoon." He felt a surge of adrenalin the instant he rang off.

The location of the secluded dwelling was clearly marked by bright white numbers painted on an arched metal placard. Clark stopped his SUV on the circular driveway fifteen feet from the entrance to the ranch-style house that seemed oddly squashed by its low-slope, black roof. The brick had been painted a blue-gray and the recessed front doors of mostly glass had narrow, shiny black frames. He jabbed the doorbell and heard movement inside.

"Come on in. Nice to meet you." Martin Cox was a dead ringer for Kevin Costner. The inside walls were a washed-out cranberry. The area rugs on the wolf-gray tile had black and blue cubes. Clark saw the built-in rifle case in the corner and pearl-handled pistol lying next to the plastic tubs in the middle of the family room.

"Is that it over there?"

"All six containers," Cox answered. He walked ahead, picked up the pistol, and tucked it in his belt. Clark took the lids off all the tubs like a surgeon prepping for an operation. Each one had similar contents: baguettes covered in bubble wrap with yellow invoices cinched around them under rubber bands.

"Is your wife at home?" he asked to make polite conversation while he took the packaging off the first item. It was a stack of ten special mint sets dated 1951. The invoice confirmed the original purchase price to be $3,605.

"Uh, no. She's in prison. Got sent up for wire fraud and writing too many opioid prescriptions. Her dad died recently and left this to her. We need to sell it, or the bank is going to take our house." He gazed at the floor, boring a hole in it with his eyes.

Clark felt the deal was already getting squirrelly, yet he thought there might be an opportunity to make some quick money on a referral. "These aren't my expertise. I can get a man out here that specializes in them."

"Could you just take it to him and bring it back with the appraisal? I trust you."

He contemplated the request, then said, "Help me load them in my vehicle."

Clark called Kelly Todd in Cape Girardeau as he left Bardwell to let him know that he would be over for a visit right at quitting time. He thought for a moment that a woman in a maroon car was following him, but dismissed the belief when he parked in front of Kelly's shop.

Todd had a profitable niche business wholesaling novelty coin offerings. His dealer network kept him busy shipping merchandise around the country night and day. In spite of that, his shop was better organized than most. "So, what have you got for me, Mister Buxton?"

"I need you to look at a big batch of stuff. I'll pay a hundred an hour for an appraisal if you'll get it done by ten in the morning."

"Big spender," he retorted. "Nice of you to show up when we're about to close. Bring it on in." By the time Clark had schlepped all six containers into the office, he was covered in sweat. Kelly took a bundle in his hand and inspected it. "What do you want me to do with all the packaging?"

"Throw it away, I guess."

"Okay, I'll make up a spreadsheet and put a value on everything. I presume you want me to price it to buy it, meaning this will be an offer?"

"Yes. If I get these, they're all yours."

Kelly worked into the night unwrapping and sorting the contents of the tubs. He then did a listing with quantities and item descriptions for everything there before knocking off for the night. He got up early the next morning and began in earnest to slog through the pricing. Near the end of the process, a four-pack of brilliantly uncirculated Peace dollars worked its way to the top of the pile. Kelly almost missed it. Three of the coins were dated 1935, and the last one read 1964. He checked the reverse for the "D" mint mark. It was there. Maybe the rumor that some had not been destroyed was true.

For the next forty-five minutes, Kelly Todd used a high-definition comparator to examine every detail of the Peace dollars with different dates. An hour later, he entered the last unit price on the list of goods to get a grand total. He punched a number in his phone and said, "The lot is worth a little over fifty-six thousand. I'll send you the spreadsheet. I put ten hours in it. You owe me a thousand dollars."

"Fifty-six thousand? Hell, the guy thinks it's worth a half a million."

Kelly responded, "Yeah, I noticed some of the values on the invoices. They were five or six times what the items are worth. This is a typical scam. These places find guys with dementia and sell junk to them until they're bled dry. The sellers are careful to send out products of some value, so they don't get arrested. Let me know if you get the deal."

Clark checked his email and opened the file that Todd had sent over. He hid the line-item detail and changed the total from $56,140 to $51,140. He printed out the appraisal and invoice for it and scanned them for accuracy. Next, he ran over to Cape, loaded up the totes, and headed to Bardwell. Martin Cox answered Clark's call with, "Well, what's the good news?"

"I don't know if it's good news or not. Your collection is worth just over fifty-one thousand."

"What? That can't be. The invoices show that her dad paid nearly three hundred thousand for everything."

"Sir, he was scammed." That was the only response he could think of.

"This is hopeless. I'm going to kill myself." The sound of a bullet being loaded in the chamber came over the line. There was a loud bang and thud before the call went dead. Clark peered at his phone in disbelief.

"Sheriff, I need someone to meet me at an address in Bardwell. I think there may have been a shooting."

Thirty minutes later, a police officer joined Buxton at the entrance to the Cox residence. The policeman squinted his eyes and rapped on the glass. He had a decidedly aggravated expression on his ruddy face. No sound came from inside the dark house. The officer reached for the door just as it was opening away from his hand. There stood Martin, in the flesh. "Come in, gentlemen. What's this about?"

The policeman said, "Mister Buxton here thought there had been a shooting at this residence."

"Certainly not. I was playing a gag on him. Check the place out for yourself." The officer left in ten minutes without saying a word to either man. "So, where are my coins?" Martin looked crazed, and Clark was perplexed.

"They're outside. I'll bring them in." He glanced over his shoulder to make sure there wasn't a pistol pointed at him.

Martin lifted the tops off the tubs and asked, "Where are the invoices that were with these?" He fanned a hand over the merchandise and stared at Clark. "After that phony appraisal you gave me, I don't trust you anymore. You're trying to con me. How do I know you didn't take a five-finger discount?"

"I didn't remove anything, nor did the guy that worked with me," Clark whimpered.

"Well, I have the pink copy of all the invoices. You better find the yellow ones that you left here with, or you'll be paying me the difference," he threatened.

"I'll get them. Your appraisal bill is fifteen hundred bucks." He thrust the papers in Martin's direction.

"Are you kidding me? I'm not paying that. Get out of here!" Martin opened the front door and shooed Clark through it. "Get those papers and bring them back in a hurry." He slammed the door so hard that the glass rattled like a crash symbol.

When Clark got in his car, he placed a call and said, "Kelly, what did you do with those yellow invoices wrapped on the coins?"

"Threw them away like you told me to," he replied.

"I need them back. This nut job is trying to pin a theft on us, and he's very handy with firearms." Kelly's stomach knotted up as he dove into the dumpster behind his shop to look for anything yellow.

He had checked the stack of invoices against what was on the spreadsheet by the time Clark walked in again. "They're all here. Everything is accounted for." He handed them over and watched his nervous friend scurry out. The car lurched away from the curb like a frustrated mule.

Clark walked back into the Cox residence and said, "Here they are."

"Let's match them up." The men used the kitchen counter to collate the sets. There were two pink invoices left, both in the amount of $10,000. "Looks like you owe me twenty-thousand dollars."

"Those weren't in there."

Martin fired back imperiously, "They were, and you or your friend must have stolen them. You can bring me the money, or I will take it out of your hide."

Clark Buxton's shoulders slumped, his mouth fell open, but no words came out. He sized Martin up for a few seconds, and when he got near the front door, he turned and declared, "You're ripping me off."

On the way back to his office, Clark called Kelly again and explained the predicament he had gotten them into. Kelly replied, "I will pay the twenty thousand and waive the appraisal charge on two conditions. First, you give me a bill of sale that states I purchased a group of coins out of the collection, and second, you get a release and hold harmless from him."

"Why would you do that?"

"Because I don't want that nut job as you call him coming after me."

Clark stepped out of his vehicle into the stifling heat after parking downtown. The acrid smell of burnt rubber from car tires assaulted his nose and upset his stomach. He threw a ring of keys down on the glass case in his shop and began preparing the documents on the computer. Twenty minutes later, he walked into the bank next door to get a check.

Martin opened the door at his house once again and said, "That was fast."

"Shall I come in?" Clark struck the pose of a fencer holding an epee.

"Certainly," Cox replied with syrupy insincerity.

"To get any money from me, you'll have to sign these." He slapped the papers on the kitchen counter and handed Martin a pen.

"Let's see the money." Martin's eyes were those of a hungry black bear. Clark waved the check at him. "I'm not taking a check. I want cash."

"This is a certified check made out to Martin Cox for twenty thousand dollars. You can sign that bill of sale and release of claims, and I'll hand it over to you. Otherwise, you can forget it. If anything happens to me, the bank has a record of this check, and the guy that helped me with the appraisal knows I'm here. Now, what's it going to be?" Cox signed the documents without reading them. Clark walked out. Within seconds, the sound of his car faded off in the distance.

Mona Cox came out of the bedroom and said to Martin, "The first part's done." He handed her the check. She took it in her hand and looked away. They searched the internet for the nearest bank branch where they could convert the check into cash. It would be a twenty-mile trip, and the bank would be closing in thirty minutes.

Clark Buxton waited for Martin to drive by before circling back to the Cox house. He had seen the woman in Martin's car and began to draw a few conclusions. Buxton used a rock to break the glass so he could reach in and unlock the front door. It took him five minutes to load the six totes of coins in his SUV for the third and final time. He drove to Kelly's shop with his sweaty shirt stuck to the back of his car seat.

"Mister Todd, I bought the whole collection from him. Here is the bill of sale and release of all claims. You don't need to front me the twenty thousand. Just give me a check for the fifty-six thousand less the thousand I owe you for the appraisal."

Kelly examined the documents carefully, then said, "I'll make a copy of these and write you a check. I don't know how you pulled it off."

By the time Clark got back to Paducah, it was nearly dark. He ducked into his favorite watering hole to order the best Kentucky straight bourbon whiskey they had. The freezing gust of air-conditioning felt good on his face. He had done it—flipped a $20,000 payout for $55,000 in two days. A grin formed on his face as he bent an elbow.

Swiss Auction No. 361

Item #37

The United States Denver Mint coined thirty test strikes and 316,076 circulation strikes of a silver Peace dollar dated 1964. The US government decided not to release the coins and made sure that all of them were destroyed. This replica is of the correct weight and silver content, and was struck from dies that yield no discernible imperfections. Interested bidders may examine the piece at the auction house under the supervision of an armed guard.

As the bidding began to heat up, the US Secret Service agent waited patiently for the first "going once" before he raised his number in the air. There was one other bidder that seemed determined to get the coin. The two men went back and forth nearly forty times until one of them relented. The US government won the bid at $889,000. After the auction fee of 10 percent and shipping costs, the seller from Monte Carlo would net right at $800,000.

When the Secret Service agent went in a private booth to take possession of the Peace dollar, the auction-house officer quipped, "You paid a lot of money for a replica."

The agent appeared annoyed. He said, "There's a law here against skiing while reciting poetry, but you can sell damn near anything you want at an auction. See any irony in that?" He stood up, took the coin, and departed.

Mona Cox parked her maroon Cadillac in front of Kelly's business several days later. She walked in and asked, "Are you Mister Todd?"

"I am. What can I do for you?"

"Are there any surveillance cameras in here?"

"Why is that?" Kelly questioned. He took a closer look at the woman who didn't appear to be a desperate criminal bent on holding him up.

"Because I need to have a private conversation with you," she answered.

"Fire away," he said. Mona Cox took two sheets of paper out of her purse and laid them on the desk.

"Those are the before and after pictures of the Peace dollars you appraised for me some time ago. You swapped out the nineteen sixty-four. I just saw where it sold at a Swiss auction for nearly nine hundred grand. If you want to buy it from me now, I won't go to the police."

Todd squirmed in his chair. "How much are you thinking?"

"Two hundred and fifty thousand."

The police were called to the Cox residence the next morning. They noted the broken glass in the front door. Martin ran to the ruddy-faced cop that had entered the house. He announced in a dispirited tone, "Someone shot my wife." Mona was lying face up, a pool of blood under her left arm socket.

The policeman cross-examined Martin with, "Several weeks ago, I met a man out here that thought there had been a shooting. Now there has been. Who was that man, and where is he? Don't touch anything until the medical examiner gets here."

Martin Cox began to tell the story. "His name is Clark Buxton. He owns Blackthorn Gold and Coin in downtown Paducah. He wouldn't have done it. The killer is most likely a guy named Kelly

Todd from Cape Girardeau. He broke in, stole a valuable coin from us, and probably wanted to keep her quiet."

What Martin didn't talk about was the two hundred and fifty thousand in cash that he had just buried at the back of the property thirty minutes before calling the police.

MOSTLY RIGHT ADVICE
FOR A GOOD LIFE

THE SPHINX

You can't buy liquor in the little town of Inez because Martin County is what is referred to as *dry*. That suited Lavan and Sarah Hanania just fine. They moved there recently from Mosul, Iraq, where intoxicating spirits were taboo unless you were awash in money. Dry counties in Kentucky were like that too.

The Hananias had been trying to immigrate to the United States for fifteen years, so when NASA offered to clear their way to the land of milk and honey, they shipped what they owned to Inez and found a practical house to buy in the country. Sarah Hanania loved the place because it was full of security cameras and came with a live-in houseman. She had grown accustomed to servants in her home back in Iraq. Ivan Ponce, a dark-skinned man, said little but could cook up a storm.

Six months ago, a high-powered Schmidt-Cassegrain telescope got assembled at the end of a meandering gravel road atop an aiguille southeast of Inez. Lavan, an astrophysicist from the University of Mosul, had been recruited to "man the store." A second staff person would join him soon to help process the endless flow of data. NASA searched its records for someone already on the payroll that might embrace the rugged Eastern Kentucky life. His name was Ratcliffe Parsons and, auspiciously, had grown up in Martin County.

Thirty years earlier, the now elderly Parsons were the backward white folks who adopted the mixed-race baby they named Ratcliffe. His birth certificate revealed he had a Caucasian father and black Cuban mother. It was rumored that the blood son of the Parsons sired the child and then left town to escape the ignominy of an interracial dalliance. "Rat" was handsome and smart. His chocolate skin had gotten lighter over the years, so much so that he now passed for white.

Rat was working at the James Clark Maxwell Telescope in Hawaii when he got the call. He had gained notoriety for his involvement in the first images of the black hole in galaxy Messier 87, and pictures of the first asteroid from another star to visit our solar system as an interstellar interloper. He surmised the best way to advance his career would be to relocate. Besides, he would be BMOC in Inez, his old stomping ground.

Lavan and Rat Parsons became fast friends soon after they developed a work routine up at the telescope. Rat visited the Hananias on Friday nights for some of Ivan's fancy food, a few hands of gin, and a bit of lively conversation. He glanced over his shoulder and asked, "Lavan, what is that ivory thing up there?" He shot a finger in the direction of the object hanging above the fireplace.

"It's a plaque of an Egyptian Sphinx from Nineveh. Mosul is near the original site of the ancient palace spoken of in the Bible and Koran. I bought it for next to nothing at a marketplace years ago." Lavan walked over and explained each feature of the artifact, and then said, "I had an expert verify its provenance."

"Is it worth anything?"

"Not really," he replied.

"We better not let my girlfriend see the thing. She'll want to do a podcast on it."

Sarah inquired, "What's her name?"

"Hendel Copeland. Just Google 'mostly right advice,' and her podcasts will pop up."

"I'll look for them," she replied.

HENDEL COPELAND

The Hendel Copeland that Rat knew in high school was a skinny, mousy urchin. By the time he came back to town, she had turned into lightning in a bottle. Her hair was now golden blond, set off by slanted, bewitching, sapphire-blue eyes. Hendel had thick sensual lips and a lithe frame that made her look like a ballerina. She ensnared Rat the moment he saw her face again, and he didn't know exactly what hit him.

Hendel had single-handedly put Inez, Kentucky, on the world stage. It started when she began producing a bootleg reality show by the name of *Virginia Side of Kentucky* that got picked up by a major network. The premise was giving advice. Anything that came up, she led with, "This is what I did," or, "This is what I'd do." The genius of the show depended on her advice being half wrong on every topic, and beyond that, much of it came across as caustic or a put-down. At least it was honest and authentic. Through the five seasons, she had grown intellectually and emotionally.

It took her a year to write a best-selling book that leveraged her propensity for telling other people what to do, aptly titled *Mostly Right Advice for a Good Life*. In the book, she gave tips on how women should talk to men and how men should act. A lot of the information was bad, but it had an Irma Bombeck quality to it. She thought her shtick was getting more serious when, in fact, it had turned comedic with the success of her book. That's what the buying public liked and wanted. To right the ship, Hendel entered the podcast world, only this time, the subject matter would be ideas and not people.

The first series of podcasts she did was on trust. Rat participated in them as the straight man, dummy, target, or whatever she told him to be. Within a couple of episodes, the repartee had devolved into an ass-kicking for him. He was relieved when she declared that the subject had been exhausted, and he would not be needed for the next series, which would be on privacy.

"Privacy, you mean like nobody knows where you are or what you're doing?" Rat baited Hendel with the question.

"It's much more than that," she pushed back.

"Well, I think you should do one on unplugging everything. You know, getting off the grid."

"I'm the one who gives advice around here, and I'm advising you to go play with your telescope and butt out." She stuck her tongue out at him, and then struck a smirk and a smile.

On the first episode of the privacy series, Hendel's beautiful face took up most of the screen as she spoke. "I'm finished with the open-concept floor plan. When I have a dinner party, I don't want the guests wandering aimlessly from the dining area to the kitchen to the den. And when I'm in the family room reading a book, I don't want to see or smell the dirty dishes piled up in the sink. Without wall space, there is no place to hide or hang pictures. You can't properly decorate wide-open space. There is something really soothing about walls, your privacy, and your own space. Listen to "In My Room" by the Beach Boys. Then you'll get it." On and on she went.

THE WIDOW

Lavan's ringing cell phone interrupted his deep, satisfying sleep. He glanced at the clock that read 4:13 a.m. NASA headquarters wanted him to run over to the telescope and shoot some coordinates at a little after five o'clock. He dressed, grabbed a muffin, climbed in his car, and sped off.

The trip up the mountain was bad enough, but the treacherous gravel road over to the facility was the part he dreaded most. He hit a rut, and the car lurched to the right. He overcorrected and careened leftward. When Lavan turned the front wheels back to the right, the left rear tire slipped off the road and started spinning angrily on the soft berm that quickly gave way. As he steered left again to straighten the fishtailing vehicle, it began to tip, and in an instant, rolled down the hill until it slammed violently into a husky oak tree. Lavan's crushed body struggled futilely for breath. He died in less than two minutes.

A month after Lavan's death, Sarah remained in a numb fog. A grief therapy firm advised her to eat regularly, and get dressed up every day. They also suggested that she postpone making any irreversible financial decisions for a while. There were calls to be made to NASA, the bank, insurance and credit card companies, not to mention the papers to go through in the office. If only she could escape from it all. Sarah lethargically typed "mostly right advice" on the computer keyboard. She opened the podcast labeled "Getting off the Grid."

"Secretly, you may have already made peace with the idea that there is no privacy. When Adam and Eve were cast out of Eden, they became painfully aware of the desire for it. Soon, Amazon and Google will know everything about you. The transmissions from the cameras in your house are stored on a cloud somewhere, and who knows who's hacking those to watch your every move. Do we want someone searching through suspicious doorbell pictures? We are building a totalitarian state that must not be allowed to stand. Even though I may lose you as a home viewer, my advice is to get off the grid. Unhook the internet, cable television, and cameras. Dump the smartphone. Find a way around it. Get an electric generator or propane tanks, put in a well, read newspapers, rent movies without giving your name, buy a fireproof safe, and clam-shell phone for emergencies, prepay for minutes, close your bank account, deal in cash, stock up on nonperishable food, and get a gun." There Hendel Copeland went again, giving half-bad advice. Most people would take it as campy or a form of dark humor. Others would certainly fall for it.

Sarah x-ed out of the podcast and sighed by exhaling slowly. The first thing she did was have the cameras in the house disconnected.

One of the grief counselors had also advised Sarah not to go into the home office at least one day a week. She ignored that. This was her tenth day in a row of reading, sorting, and throwing papers away. Then she found an interesting piece of correspondence from an art dealer in London, which read:

Dear Lavan Hanania,

I wanted to let you know that the Ivory Sphinx you own is a very valuable artifact. It is not listed as one of the stolen pieces relative to the fall of Saddam Hussein, thus would not be within the purview of any governing body if sold privately. To that end, my offer to purchase the Sphinx for one million US dollars is open-ended, with no expiration date. Please contact me if you wish to arrange a transaction.

Sincerely,

Dane Ferber

The best thing to do now, she mused, was to drive over to Lexington and find a financial advisor that she could trust to organize her affairs the way she wanted them. After that, she would sell the Sphinx and move out of Martin County. Sarah let Ivan know that she would be gone for a few days. He nodded and went back to scrubbing the dirt off of a large beet.

IVAN PONCE

"So, who is this Ivan Ponce that lives with Sarah Hanania?" Hendel directed the question at Rat, who sat in a rocking chair with one booted leg propped on the other.

"I don't know. He came with the house when they bought it. I know this, he's a hell of a cook and card player." Rat uncrossed his leg and leaned forward.

"That's what I'm after. I'd like to steal him from her. Is there any chance of that?"

"I don't think she'll stay around very much longer. There's nothing here for her."

"Before I try, would you check him out?"

Rat gave in and said, "Why not. Maybe I'll come across some juicy gossip." He got up and waved to Hendel as he hoofed it to his car. The first stop he made was at the Ponce farm nine miles northwest of town. The grizzled black man he talked to provided him with some information that would have to be run down.

Ivan finished eating leftovers and proceeded to the office to watch one of Hendel Copeland's podcasts on privacy. He clicked on "God Knows Your Secrets."

"Privacy is equated to darkness and evil, at least those are the metaphors Saint Paul used. It abets sin. Nothing is hidden that will not be seen by God. Everything that is exposed by the light becomes visible. But what about your spiritual life? Isn't that supposed to be private? Sure it is. Public displays of piety are distasteful. To grow, you must try and fail, learn from your failings and sins. One of those sins is checking your blasted phone every two or three minutes. If you said a prayer every two or three minutes, you'd be better off . . ."

A bicycle rider approached the Hanania property in the dark. He was completely covered in black tights except for narrow eye slits. He parked his bike facing the driveway and used a key to get into the house. The intruder tiptoed to the fireplace and threw something on it before reaching up for the Ivory Sphinx. He crept back to the front door and yelled, "Hey, Ivan!" He jumped on the bike and pedaled off quickly with the plaque under one arm.

Ivan reached for the pistol in the desk drawer and kept still. He knew better than to walk into a trap. After a few minutes, he went into the family room and turned on the light. Ivan looked at the fireplace and stroked his chin. He looked outside, relocked the front door, and went to bed.

The Martin County Sheriff, Doby Kirkland, sat in the living room at the Hanania house along with Sarah and Ivan. "So, how did it happen, Ivan?" he asked.

"I don't know. I heard somebody yell my name. I went into the family room to see who it was and noticed that the Sphinx was gone. I looked out the front door and saw nothing."

"Did you recognize the voice?"

"I'm not sure. It sounded like Rat Parsons."

Sarah said, "Well, I hope my insurance company will cover the loss. The thing was worth at least a million dollars."

Kirkland got up and went over to the fireplace and put his face close to the brick. He pointed and said, "Wonder what that is? It looks like blood." He turned to face Ivan. "Do you know anything about this?"

"No."

"Ivan, we're going to need to get your DNA. I'll subpoena Rat Parsons for his."

The results came back a week later that showed the blood matched Ivan's DNA. Kirkland went back out to Sarah's house right after lunch. "Ivan, I'm afraid I don't believe your story. The blood on the fireplace is yours. You must have cut yourself pulling that thing off the wall. I'm going to have to arrest you."

All Ivan could say was, "I didn't do it."

DOUBLE JEOPARDY

Rat's DNA results came in four days before Ivan's trial. Kirkland's first call was to the lab to verify that something hadn't gone wrong with the samples. He then began searching through records. The next morning, the sheriff arrested Parsons for stealing the Ivory Sphinx.

"Judge, we have an interesting case here. Both men deny doing the crime, yet both men's DNA are present at the crime scene. So, one of them must have done it."

The judge asked, "What evidence do we have?"

"None, other than the DNA." Kirkland tossed what he had in his hand on the table.

"Well, if both men's DNA are present, you should charge both of them with the crime."

"That's the problem, Judge. These men have the same DNA. We don't know which one did it."

"What do you mean they have the same DNA? That's not possible."

"It is if they're identical twins, and they are. I checked their birth certificates." Ivan and Rat, sitting together, turned to look at each other.

"How can that be? One of the men looks white and the other black?"

"I'm not a doctor, Judge," Kirkland responded.

"If there's no other evidence against either one of them, then we can't identify which one of them did it. Case dismissed." The gavel whapped immediately, startling the crowd.

Fortunately for Sarah Hanania, her insurance company paid the claim on the Ivory Sphinx less a sizable deductible. She had decided to relocate to Louisville because it was the biggest city in Kentucky, a place where she could keep busy with lots of activities. Ivan had planned to stay with the house once it sold, but a better offer came his way.

Rat sat in Hendel's rocking chair, reading a newspaper. She asked him, "How much did you get for the Sphinx?"

"Pardon me?"

"Come on, Rat. I know you stole it."

"What proof do you have?" He seemed a little nervous now.

"Ivan tells me that you told Sarah to start watching my podcasts, and you're the one that put the idea in my head to do an episode on getting off the grid. I encouraged people to unhook their security cameras, and that's exactly what she did."

"Circumstantial evidence," Rat declared. "What about double jeopardy?"

"There's more. My cousin owns a key-making machine over in Paintsville. He recognized you from one of my podcasts. He called to let me know that you had just been through to get a key made. He wanted to make sure I knew about it in case the key was to something of mine. If I tell the sheriff about that, you're toast."

Rat propped his head on his thumb and first finger. "How do we fix this?"

"How much did you get for the Sphinx?"

"Enough."

"Rat, I'm going to give you some advice that's not mostly right, but dead-on. Ivan will never have the opportunity to make the kind of money you can. I say you put five hundred thousand in cash in a suitcase and give it to him."

"Consider it done." The sweat on Rat's forehead and upper lip were visible from across the room.

Hendel hollered over her shoulder, "Ivan, would you bring Mister Parsons a tall bourbon with two large ice cubes?" Two minutes later, Ivan appeared, glass in hand. That was the first time anybody had ever seen him smile.

THE SWEET SCIENCE CAN MAKE YOUR HEAD ACHE

No one seriously disputed the fact that The Black Pearl made the best clam chowder in the world. Just ask Noah Thorp. He tended bar there six nights a week. Even though he made an excellent living as a bartender, Noah really wanted to be a chef.

He was passionate about three things: cooking, boxing, and chasing women. Anda Solomonov, the woman he chased and caught, for the time being, was a brooding, black-haired, black-eyed girl from a family of chefs and restaurateurs. She waitressed at "the Pearl" and talked of running her own quaint little bistro someday.

Noah placed $500 in Anda's hand and primed her with, "Go in the kitchen and don't come back without the recipe for that clam chowder."

Three minutes later, Anda walked behind the bar, pulled on Noah's belt, and stuffed a piece of paper down the back of his pants. "That'll cost you more than five hundred," she quipped.

When Noah graduated from high school, he jumped straight into the boxing business. He was plenty mean enough back then and had the heart to be a great boxer, but didn't have the tools to be exceptional. He spent ten years working his way up the circuit and back down again.

During that time, he did become exceptional at conning women. What else was he to do with all that spare time on his hands? Learning how to cook came to mind. It took him nearly three years to get his associate's degree in culinary arts. Noah stuck with bartending, though, because of the money. Occasionally, he did apply for a higher-paying chef job requiring a bachelor's degree and some experience. He had neither.

Noah finally received a serious reply from a restaurant in Helsinki, seeking an American chef that could bring new recipes to the table. They urged him to send something over for them to try. It might have been a come on to fleece eager chefs, but he took a flyer. Enter one fabulous recipe for clam chowder. He got hired, said bye to Anda, and moved to Finland forthwith.

The Nordic surname of Thorp buoyed Noah's street cred as a chef for a while. His paucity of original recipes beyond clam chowder eventually relegated him to obscurity that turned into disillusionment. Another way to skin the cat, he thought, was to try boxing again. He went to Tarmo on Sturenkatu to pick up a few fights and sparring gigs for extra money. That lasted until headaches flared up every time Noah took a punch. Since he couldn't get in the ring anymore, he at least intended to be a serious historian of the sport. That's when he began collecting videos of famous fights.

Noah was also illicitly collecting recipes by the best Finnish chefs. He checked the menus of the finer spots in town and bribed the help at those restaurants to slip him the ingredients and methods for cooking their world-class dishes. When he tried to pay off the wrong person, he had to vanish in the dead of night to save his skin. He dialed an old flame's cell number and said soothingly, "Anda, honey, it's Noah. Where are you?"

She paused before giving him a deadpan reply, "Kentucky. I'm working in the kitchen at a horse farm."

"I'm coming home. Why don't you find us a little place where we can open our own bistro? I've got some of the best recipes in the world now. You can make that dream of yours come true."

"How romantic," she answered caustically.

Midway, Kentucky, had only three noteworthy restaurants for the longest time. Now it had five. The little enclave was midway between Frankfort and Lexington, and midway between Versailles and Georgetown. It also happened to be in the heart of thoroughbred breeding and bourbon distilling country. One would have expected it to have been densely populated. It wasn't. There hadn't been any real growth there since the railroad came through in the early 1800s. What it did have nearby were peregrine horse and whiskey VIPs tramping around looking for good places to eat.

One of the two new restaurants in town had the name Amiata Senza, which loosely meant "without lava" in Italian. The upscale eatery was located in a rezoned one-story farmhouse. Eschewing equestrian prettification had been a calculated risk. The exterior looked dull with its wood planks, rusty nails, and weathered steel. Inside, the floors were paved in gray porcelain cotto tiles, and the room enclosures had been slathered with a sienna and oxide-rich whitewash. A mural of stars and constellations adorned the ceilings. Japanese and Chinese plates of maroon and yellow hung in abundance throughout. The walnut tables had curved-back chairs, and the chinoiserie was chopped up by intermittent Umbrian cupboards.

The restaurant featured wild game, sheep cheese, local honey, spiced pumpkin seeds, chicory, and wines made from Sangiovese and Pinot Grigio grapes. The executive chef and proprietor, Natalie Antonelli, ran selections of daikon radish and grapefruit over quince and black garlic, rice cakes in mussel broth kicked up by a dollop of salmon roe, shitake mushrooms in chicken-broth aspic drizzled with chili oil, and crunchy fingerling potatoes smothered in sour cream and buttery oyster mushrooms. Her signature dish was a Jerusalem Grill of boneless chicken thighs and livers with red onions, lemon, turmeric, cumin, fenugreek, and cinnamon.

Natalie started working in her father's Baltimore restaurant at the age of fourteen. After many years, she struck out on her own and became the Executive Chef for the Maryland Jockey Club at Pimlico Race Course. On numerous occasions, famous horsemen would eat at the club and comment on how they wished she would come to Kentucky so they could partake in her fine fare more often. That's what she eventually did. It took her six months to ready the Midway property for a New Year's Day opening.

On Valentine's Day, Natalie left the kitchen early and ducked into a cozy bar on Main Street. It was singles night. The bouncer gave her a number, and she noticed that some sort of Valentine's game was underway. The idea was for guests to send each other Valentine's using numbers instead of names. If the receiver wanted to meet the sender, then a note back to them signaled so. The first Valentine Natalie got came from number four. It read, "Be my Valentine, and I'll prepare you the finest meal you've ever eaten." She looked around the room and spotted him. The man was ruggedly handsome, a physical specimen. He raised his glass to her when she looked his way. Her note back to him said, "Come over and introduce yourself."

"I'm Noah Thorp." He had enough manners to know that one didn't offer to shake hands with a woman unless she offered first, which she didn't.

"Natalie Antonelli."

"Oh, you're the owner of Amiata Senza. I've been meaning to come by and see you. I just opened Sweet Science across town two weeks ago. Can you believe it, two new restaurants in a little town like this?"

"I'm so busy, we've been turning people away every night," she said.

"Us too. A good problem to have, I guess. How about that meal offer I made for your Valentine?" he asked with the sappiness of a begging pet.

"What day are you closed?"

"Monday."

"Me too. Want to do it then? I presume you meant at your restaurant, right?" She wanted to gather as much intelligence about the competition as she could.

"Monday it is. I'll meet you there at six."

Sweet Science appeared to be an elongated hexagonal structure with a Mediterranean-blue entrance door in the middle of a tomato-soup-colored front wall. The kitchen took up the back third of the building. A whimsical skylight roof had many shades of sparkling stained glass. In the center of the dining room, a display case elegant enough for the Hope Diamond held a classic red-and-blue plastic Rock'Em Sock'Em boxing toy for kids. Two of the four walls were shelved with videos of famous fights. The spines of the binders had fight numbers and names on them. The other two gray walls were covered with promotional fight posters and slicks of great pugilists. The antique white tables and brown velvet chairs had a ringside feel.

Thorp built an impressive food offering amalgamated from other chefs. His recommended feature was any kind of seafood glazed with sweet and smoky pomegranate molasses. The basics in many dishes were root vegetables, herbs, berries, hard cheeses, and forage fish. His signature dish included a thin slice of arctic turnip rolled around a creamy filling of whitefish drizzled in dill oil topped with whitefish roe along with walnut and red pepper paste in fruity olive oil over braised eggplant, tomatoes and tiny chickpeas. The wine offerings were made from Nebbiolo and Sauvignon Blanc grapes.

When Natalie walked in the front door of Sweet Science, she saw Noah through the mail-slot opening in the wall of the kitchen. He looked up to acknowledge her, then down again to get back to preparing their dinner. A single table had been set for two with wine and silverware. "Nice place you have here, Noah. I see you like boxing." She craned her neck backward to take in the kooky skylight above her head.

"Yes, I boxed for many years. Now I like to watch great fights."

Noah served Natalie an impressive meal that she acknowledged as such, and they exchanged stories of their pasts. He cleared the dishes and brought out decaf coffee. In his left hand, he held an Extra-Strength Excedrin bottle that had a piece of masking tape on it. Written in black marker was: *For Noah Only.* He flipped open the top and popped three of the tablets without any water. "I get headaches now an again. Too many punches in my boxing days, I guess."

"That's no fun." Natalie showed sympathy and kept quiet for a minute. "Can I ask if you've got any partners?"

"Yes. My girlfriend Anda. She has the money, and I've got the recipes."

Girlfriend! What the hell is this lothario doing sending Valentines out when he's got a girlfriend? Dollars to donuts, he's a bigtime chaser. "Well, that answers a couple of questions," she said with resignation.

"Not really." He undressed her with his eyes. "Say, can I ask a favor of you? On opening weekend at Keeneland in six weeks, a party at the Show Barn is going to feature the food of four local restaurants. I'm going to do it. Two other restaurants have been picked, and they want me to suggest a third. Would you like to participate? The common menu items will be burbot and celeriac. I have plenty of recipes if you need them. They're giving out a prize for the tastiest item."

Natalie knew of Keeneland from her days at Pimlico. It sounded like a good way to break into the horse crowd. Maybe one of her former customers would recognize her there. "Sure, I'll do it," she said.

"Great! I hope to get a chance to enjoy your fine food soon," he responded pleasantly.

She wasn't offering anything. The guy seemed slimy all of a sudden. "Thanks for the delicious meal. You certainly have the knack." As she walked out of the restaurant, the eyes of the fighters in the posters were on her, their fists poised to punch her with glee.

Two days later, Natalie closed Amiata and walked out to her car at ten o'clock. Under the windshield wiper was a note card that read, "You're the prettiest lady in these parts. Will you be my Valentine?" That's all it said. She heard a car speed by and thought it looked like Noah. The next day when she left her house for work, the same car drove by again. Another note card had the words, "Hope you have a wonderful day!"

Natalie dialed the Sweet Science phone number, and said, "This is Miss Antonelli over at Amiata Senza. Is this Anda?"

"It is."

"Would you be willing to meet me for breakfast tomorrow morning in Lexington? Waffle House on Paris Pike at nine?"

"Yeah." She hung up.

Anda seemed surprisingly pleasant to Natalie as they made small talk amongst the construction workers, truck drivers, and forlorn waitresses. "So, what's on your mind?" Anda asked.

"I think Noah is stalking me." Natalie shifted and took a sip of coffee.

"Wouldn't surprise me. I used to work with him when he was a bartender. He had them coming and going. He doesn't respond very well to being ignored."

"I think he's been leaving notes on my car."

"How romantic." Anda apparently used that line frequently.

"He told me you were his girlfriend. Is that the case?"

"What do you think? I'm in business with him. I've been to bed with him. I've always wanted to have my own restaurant. I needed him to establish the kitchen. If our place is a success, I'll be able to go it alone when he's gone."

"You'll do well. I want you to know that I'm all for you. If I can help in any way, please call me."

Anda seemed to soften a bit. She added, "Thanks."

A chilly wind whistled through the Show Barn at Keeneland. April weather in Kentucky could be cruel at the most inopportune time. The four restaurants had their food stands set up in the corners of the room. Burbot, a prehistoric fish, was known as "po' man's lobster." Natalie had prepared hers on a bed of seaweed, turnip foam, and yellow beets. Noah and Anda put a buttery sauce over the opaline fish and placed it on spiced carrots, caraway, and lemony lavage pesto.

Each station had a prepared side and dessert. Sweet Science presented its celeriac in a cream sauce flavored with pine-bark vinegar, and the pastry was made with red bean paste and fruit topped with lingonberry ice cream. Amiata Senza did the celeriac in pickled horseradish, and the dessert was a heavy almond cake with spruce-scented meringue.

The food went fast, and there were compliments all around. A committee of six men and women huddled by the door to pick the best dish of the soiree. The leader of the group approached the podium and asked for the attention of the crowd. "Folks, we've picked a winner. I want to thank all four restaurants that put in the effort to make this event enjoyable for all of us. Everything tasted so good that we had a tough time singling anything out. We all agreed that the fish entrée from Sweet Science was particularly delicious. Don't y'all agree?" A half-hearted clap came from the people listening with one ear. "Noah Thorp, would you come up and accept your prize? It's a bottle of fine Kentucky bourbon from the Van Winkle family." That brought a more enthusiastic chorus of oohs and aahs.

Noah appeared sluggish as he grasped the whiskey bottle in his hand. When he stepped up to the microphone, he gazed out over the long wooden dining table with vacant eyes and a hollow expression. "I….I…," he muttered, and then fell forward, taking the podium with him. The whiskey bottle flew out of his hand and exploded on the edge of the table. Several screams dampened the thuds of his fall. Noah landed on his back, eyes open and mouth agape. He was stone-cold dead and could not be resuscitated.

The police ushered Natalie Antonelli into an interrogation room the next morning. The two detectives gestured for her to sit before they took seats across from her. "So, we understand that Mister Thorp may have been stalking you, is that right?"

"Somebody was. It might have been him. What exactly did he die from?"

"Well, we don't have the autopsy report yet, but he had an Excedrin bottle in his pocket that contained cyanide. We suspect that he was poisoned."

"I've seen that bottle. Did it say for Noah only?" Natalie asked. If she was nervous, it didn't show.

The younger of the two men pulled an envelope out of his coat pocket. "It did. He also had this on him. Does it mean anything to you?" The sheet inside read:

Fight #671
Anda Solomonov vs. Noah Thorp
Keeneland Show Barn

Natalie studied the paper, looked away, grinned slightly, and shook her head slowly. "This must have been some kind of joke he was playing on Anda. The shelves at Sweet Science are covered with videos of fights that have this kind of information on the spine of the binder; the fight number, fighters, and location."

"Thanks for your time, Miss Antonelli," replied the older detective as the two men exited the room, leaving her there to find her way out.

The younger detective rejoined his partner three hours later in the video room. He opened the plastic holder, took out the disc, and inserted it into the DVD player. He said, "I found it on the wall at the restaurant."

The screen featured a woman looking at a pill bottle on a shelf. She removed it and dumped the pills out into her hand, and then placed them on the counter. She took another pill bottle out of her pocket, put those pills in the first bottle, and shoveled the pills on the counter into the second one. She put the first bottle back on the shelf and walked out of frame with the second bottle before the screen went black.

"Who's the woman?" asked the older detective.

"Anda Solomonov. Thorp must have secretly filmed her setting him up to be poisoned."

"Then why would he be dumb enough to take the pills?"

"I don't know. Maybe there was some other switch later on."

"Let's wait for the toxicology report before we pick her up."

Two days later, Natalie sat in the interrogation room again. She asked, "What have you found out about Noah's death?"

"He died of an aneurism. There was no poison in his system. Can you think of any reason why he would film Anda Solomonov trying to poison him?"

She shifted her eyes back and forth between the detectives. "Blackmail. He was afraid that she would boot him out for being a philanderer. Looks like she's in the clear now." Natalie got up and left the room. On the way to her car, she raised a phone to her ear, and said, "Anda, the louse died of an aneurism. I'm coming by so we can figure out how to find you a better chef, one that isn't a headache."

Hey, Hey, What Did You Do?

MARTY COLNON

The real estate business is a bit of a beauty contest. A successful agent has to look pretty, bright-eyed, and honest. Marty Colnon had the bright-eyed part going for him. He was a short, florid Irishman with an ill-fitting gray toupee that never seemed to properly blend into his tonsure. He wore the same style of clothing day after day, a collarless black shirt and Italian Oxford pants cinched in by a shiny black belt with a curved, mirrored buckle. The Figaro silver chain around his neck had a leather pouch hanging from it that held a vapor stick for on-the-spot nicotine consumption. He would have made it big in Las Vegas, but this was Newport, Kentucky. He was starving.

The hillside town of Newport that overlooked Cincinnati from the south side of the Ohio River had undergone gentrification for forty years. The new Monadnock Apartments were slow to lease out though, which presented Marty with an opportunity he couldn't pass up. He moved into a big unit himself and leased ten one-bedroom apartments under ten different names, stocking them with enough furniture for comfortable habitation. He posted the apartments on MetroBnb under false host names to avoid the suspicion of running an illegal hotel ring. It wasn't long before the cash flow from the rentals afforded him a comfortable lifestyle.

To impress the few friends Marty had, he made a sweet deal with the bartender at the Sloppy Kiss. He bought empty Pappy Van Winkle bourbon bottles for three hundred bucks and filled them with Eagle Rare. No one would know the difference, so he thought.

DECLAN COETZEE

Declan Coetzee hailed from South Africa. He sold his stake in a diamond mine for ten million dollars before the government started confiscating personal property without compensating the owners. He flew into Cincinnati the first time he visited the US because it was the closest big airport to horse country. Declan was obsessed with thoroughbred racing, and for no particular reason, the Cincinnati Reds professional baseball team caught his fancy. He fell into a pattern of wintering in his homeland and summering in Kentucky. He breezed in at the end of March to catch the Reds opening day, and returned to South Africa in mid-November after the Breeders' Cup.

Declan rented a unit in the Monadnock Apartments that overlooked Great American Ball Park, the stadium where the Reds played on the north side of the Ohio River. He carefully furnished his unit with impressive books, artwork, and liquor because he could. The place appeared dated, homey, and inviting to the several lady friends that he entertained. Marty Colnon lived across the hall.

AMBER AND DAVIS ROSALES

Amber began reading voraciously at the age of twelve and became a full-blown bibliophile by her early twenties. Being an introvert, she found the secret to snagging a husband was joining a New York City book club. Amber met Davis at a klatch. She was astonished to learn that he read more than she did. He liked non-fiction while she preferred mysteries and bodice rippers. They married based on a complimentary love of books that quickly escalated into the pastime of collecting rare first editions by American authors. This pursuit gave them a way to travel the country, attend auctions, and see the sights of a new city.

Amber inexplicably got sick of reading and quit altogether. When she shared that fact with Davis, he scolded and derided her unmercifully. Something died inside her that never came alive again after that tongue-lashing. She put up with his condescension and began planning how she could get her hands on a pile of cash before walking out on the imperious, pompous bastard.

Davis Rosales, along with the Nagys, arranged a couples trip to Cincinnati to participate in an auction that featured an unproofed manuscript of Vonnegut's classic novel, *Slaughterhouse Five*. He found two places to rent on MetroBnb. Because of a glitch in the registration system, both couples were confirmed for the same apartment, number five eleven.

YARMILLA AND WENZEL NAGY

Yarmilla and Wenzel met at the Met. He said something about a Thomas Hart Benton oil that she felt compelled to expound on. A romance struck up between them. Both were of Romanian descent. What they had in common, driving them to marry, was a passion for collecting modern art. She worked in a law office in Manhattan. He owned a sketchy little locksmith business. Wenzel came off as pusillanimous and diffident, but was far from it. Yarmilla wore the pants at home. On the job, however, Wenzel had a fearless streak in him that the police appreciated and leveraged when it came to defeating bothersome locks.

The art collecting quickly got out of hand as Wenzel saw it. Yarmilla woke up every morning yearning for that fix, a new piece of art to buy that would satisfy. The latest targets were pieces by Andre Butzer and Norman Akers that were going up for sale at the auction in Cincinnati. She borrowed $100,000 from the bank, insisting that Wenzel sign on the loan too. That was the last straw for him. He was going to somehow scrape together $50,000, pay off his half of the loan, and then decamp.

TROUBLE IN RIVER CITY

Declan stepped across the hall and knocked on the plum-tone, lacquered door that had a brass escutcheon on it with the numbers six-three-two. "Come on in," Marty responded as his nominal neighbor complied with the request.

"I wanted to ask you a favor. I'm going back to South Africa for the winter and was hoping that you could check in on my place maybe once a month to make sure everything is okay." Declan had his finger through the key ring and was twirling it. "I know you have several units in this building, so this sort of thing might not be too much of an inconvenience for you."

"Not at all. Glad to do it." Marty hoped the news of his enterprise wasn't widespread.

"This is the key, and here is my cell phone number. Call me if anything needs attending to. I'll be leaving in the morning." He handed him a calling card and the key ring.

"I certainly will," Marty confirmed. "Have a safe trip."

That evening, the Rosaleses and Nagys went through the protocol for getting into their rented apartments in Newport. They noticed the same unit number on each reservation and were momentarily stymied. Davis had the presence of mind to call the emergency phone number provided on the paperwork. A man answered, "Marty, here."

"Yes, this is Davis Rosales. I reserved two apartments on MetroBnb under the names Rosales and Nagy, and it seems that both confirmations are for the same spot. Can you get us a second apartment?"

"Just a moment. Let me check the reservations." Marty went to his computer to investigate the problem. All ten apartments he managed were rented. "I'm sorry for the mistake. There are no other units available tonight. I can find other accommodations for you."

Davis responded, "We've already paid for this location. We don't want other accommodations."

Marty panicked for a second. "Well, I don't have another solution. Wait. One of you come up to six thirty-two. I'll put you in six thirty-three across from me."

"My wife and I will be right up."

Marty ushered Amber and Davis through Coetzee's apartment door. He darted around to make sure there wasn't anything personal lying about. The place was immaculate, and it reminded him of a sixties bachelor's pad—blond-wood floors, cherry art-deco furniture, a plush green area rug, loaded bookshelves, colorful artwork on the walls, and a fully fitted kitchen and bar. The muted downtown lights coming through the diaphanous sheers in the living room formed a night mood that was hard to describe or duplicate.

"This place is really nice," Amber said.

"Here's the key. Call me when you're getting ready to check out. I'll get it back from you." Marty set the key ring on the kitchen counter and said, "Enjoy your stay."

Amber put the phone to her ear, saying, "Come to six thirty-three, you guys and check this place out." She scanned the bookshelf and saw what she hoped Davis wouldn't see—first editions of *The Great Gatsby* and *The Maltese Falcon*.

Yarmilla and Wenzel met Amber and Davis in Coetzee's upscale digs. Yarmilla wanted to party, Wenzel not so much. He did notice the two paintings on the wall, which looked to be original works by Helen Frankenthaler. The couples raided Declan's bar and helped themselves to a good bottle of wine. They engaged in a little cultural badinage on art in general, went over the logistics for attending tomorrow's auction, and then split up for the night after finishing their drinks.

Wenzel fired up his laptop in bed to search the catalog of Frankenthaler works. He found the paintings quickly. They were both considered untitled pieces, one from 1966 and the other from 1968.

The auction the couples attended the next day was a bust. The items they had an interest in went off at exorbitant prices. Some well-heeled, corpulent hillbilly gobbled up nearly everything at a fifty percent premium. Davis made sure to accidentally on purpose kick the man's chair leg on the way out of the bidding hall. The couples agreed to find a place within walking distance of the Monadnock to drown their sorrows. They fought off the November wind and trekked over to the Sloppy Kiss.

When Davis and Yarmilla went to the restroom, Amber spoke softly to Wenzel. "I noticed there are first edition books by Scott Fitzgerald and Dashiell Hammett in our apartment."

"Yeah, I saw them. Did Davis see them?"

"Not yet. He's a self-absorbed ass. He reads nonfiction. What a bore."

"How do you really feel?" Wenzel mocked her to blunt her anger.

As Yarmilla and Davis were walking back to the table, he said, "You know, Amber doesn't read anymore."

She gave him an alluring smile and replied, "That's too bad."

The four New Yorkers ate bar food and got reasonably pixelated before heading back to the Monadnock for the evening. The next morning, Wenzel brought the rental car around front and waited for the other three to join him for the ride to the airport.

"Here is the key to the unit. I must say, this apartment was worth twice what we paid," Amber offered. Marty looked the place over carefully, and the only distressful thing he noticed was the empty Silver Oak bottle in the trash.

"I hope you had a nice time," Marty commented as he followed them out.

On the way to the airport, Wenzel announced, "I'm going to delay my return to New York by a couple of days. I want to visit a college friend of mine that lives in Dayton."

Yarmilla asked, "Who's that, honey?"

"Tony Orton. He came to our wedding." Tony was a college friend, but didn't live in Dayton. He lived in Portofino, Italy.

"Yes, I remember. Well, I guess I'll see you when you get home then." Yarmilla really didn't care much what he did. She wanted to get back to New York to scour the art galleries for another purchase. After all, she had $100,000 in her checking account.

Marty bought a replacement bottle of Silver Oak for Declan's bar. When he placed it in the liquor cabinet, he saw them and damn near fainted: six bottles of gold-wax Pappy Van Winkle. They were going for $8,999 a bottle on the internet. He shut the cabinet door and began to look around the living room at the books and paintings, wondering how much they were worth. He needed to get out of there and stay out, which he did for at least the rest of that day.

Wenzel parked the rental car on a side street above the Monadnock at a little before midnight. He entered the apartment building with a group of young tenants that paid no attention to him. He took the stairs to the sixth floor and put his ear to 632, hearing nothing. Wenzel turned to 633 and inserted the paper clip tension wrench into the bottom of the keyhole. He applied clockwise pressure while inserting the bobby-pin rake in the top. He jiggled the rake up and down to scoop each pin upward until the lock released and the door opened. It was a little before one in the morning when he finally got back to his hotel room carrying an oversized, flat bag.

Wenzel's plan was to ship the stolen merchandise to his business address in New York. He would dump the stuff at a discount and pay off half of the loan. He looked at the two books first. The jackets may have been real, but the books weren't. Next, he flipped the artwork over to inspect the backside of the canvases. The cloth looked brand new. The paintings were recent copies. The whole lot might be worth a $1,000. Only one person in the world would think the stuff was worth more than that. Wenzel reached in his pocket to retrieve his dated Monadnock apartment reservation. At the bottom was the emergency number that Davis had called.

The next morning, Wenzel walked to the hotel next door. He used the house phone to dial the number. The man that answered said, "This is Marty."

"Marty, I have two books and two paintings that came out of six thirty-three. They're worth a quarter of a million dollars, but because I'm a nice guy, I'll sell them to you for fifty thousand." There was silence. "Marty?"

"Who is this?"

"Warren Buffet."

"What makes you think I want to buy them?" Marty's throat tightened.

"Economics. Pay me fifty, or you'll be paying the owner two fifty."

"It's his loss, not mine."

Wenzel set the hook with, "I saw some people partying in that unit two nights ago. I know the owner is gone. He's not a man to be trifled with. You broke the rules."

"Oh, man," Marty whimpered.

"Bring fifty thousand in cash to the parking lot of The Party Source at noon today. Park near the middle. Get out and hold up the envelope with the cash in it. You'll see a trunk pop up. I'll meet you there, and we'll do a trade. Don't pull anything you'll regret."

Marty went into 633 to confirm that the books and paintings were actually missing. He extracted $50,000 from the safe in his apartment before taking the elevator to street level. He had not physically seen Wenzel, or wasn't aware that Wenzel had been a renter, so he didn't recognize him when they made the switch that took all of forty seconds. Marty put the books on the shelf and rehung the pictures in Declan's apartment as soon as he got back to the Monadnock. He exhaled and staggered back across the hall to pour himself a stiff drink. His devious mind began to craft scenarios for getting back his $50,000 as the effects of the alcohol hit him.

AIN'T NOTHING LIKE THE REAL THING, BABY

Marty had it figured out. He would fill six of his Pappy bottles with Eagle Rare, dip the tops in dull gold wax and swap them out for the real ones in Coetzee's liquor cabinet. Maybe the bartender at the Sloppy Kiss would buy them. Might as well try to sell them now and worry about making up and placing the fakes later.

The bartender's name at the Sloppy Kiss was Aguinaldo, but he went by the sobriquet "Aggie." He saw Marty clomp into the bar carrying the gold-wax specimens in a six-pack wine bag. Aggie recognized them right off. "Where'd you get those?" he asked as his hands worked away like a robot's.

"Tooth fairy. How much will you give me for them?"

"Eight thousand a piece if they're real."

"What do you mean, real?"

Aggie shot Marty a pesky smirk. "Counterfeit Pappy is where it's at, man. Set those babies up here on the bar. Let me see if they're authentic." Aggie took them out of the bag and lined them up on the back wall. He opened a pantry and retrieved a wand that had a purple bulb in it.

"What are you doing?" Marty asked.

"Making sure I haven't seen these bottles before." He plugged the black light in and switched it on. When he ran the wand down the face of the first bottle, he stopped at the bottom for a second. Aggie checked the rest of the bottles the same way. He turned to face Marty and roared, "Hey, hey, what did you do? These bottles belong to Declan Coetzee."

"What? How do you know that?"

"Because I sold them to him. They're fake. I get five hundred for a fake bottle with booze in it, and three hundred for empties. You know that because you buy empties from me. All the bottles I sell are fake."

"How do you know those are Declan's?"

Aggie shined the black light on the bottom of the label. The initials DC were visible in neon purple. "I stamp all of the bottles I sell with the initials of the buyer. That way, I can tell who's conning whom. All the empty bottles I've sold you are stamped MC." He put the bottles in the tote and said, "You better put these back in Declan's apartment to go along with all of the other fake stuff he has in there."

"What are you talking about?" Marty questioned.

"You know, the books and the paintings, and all the other crap. It's all phony. I'm sure he did it to impress the right woman someday."

Wenzel picked up his bag and walked down to the curb at LaGuardia. As he opened Amber's car door, Yarmilla and Davis stepped out of the terminal. Yarmilla snapped a picture of them with her phone and called out, "Hey, hey, what are you doing?"

"Leaving you for her." He pointed at Amber. All Davis did was frown.

Yarmilla threw her phone at Wenzel and hit him on the kneecap. "Davis is twice the man you'll ever be," she spat.

"I'm going to the bank tomorrow to pay down your loan by fifty thousand. You can eat the rest." Wenzel kicked Yarmilla's phone away, got in Amber's car, and slammed the door. Amber flipped her off and stepped on the gas.

Bad Times of Garth Baldwin

TWENTY-SEVEN HOURS AGO

The jovial man launched himself into Ten Furlongs bar intending to sell a story of success he'd had at Keeneland a few hours earlier. He was tall, brown haired, brown eyed, and wore a pasty tan suit trimmed out with a burnt orange and pea green foulard tie and handkerchief. There were two pins on his lapel, one showing the crest of the Clubhouse and the other heralding the slogan "Go, Inky, Go".

"Hey, bartender, pour me the best bourbon you got, and put it over ice." He flipped two fingers forward and dropped his head in a call to action.

"That would be Pappy Van Winkle twenty year old at ninety dollars a shot," the bartender warned.

"Then pour one for yourself. I'm paying. I just won twenty-eight thousand, nine hundred and thirty dollars on a straight trifecta at the track." The bartender put two glasses of ice on the bar and filled both with the finest known brown liquor in the world. The lucky gambler looked side to side and furtively took a sip before chugging the rest. He crashed the glass down on the bar and said, "Tasty. I'll have another." The bartender shoved forward the glass he had filled for himself and pulled away the empty one.

"Shall I run a tab? So far, you're two hundred and seventy in."

The man deftly slipped his right hand into his trouser pocket and extracted a stockpile of folded bills. He threw three hundreds up on the bar. "Keep the change. Say, I'm feeling lucky. Know anywhere I can play a pick three lottery ticket?"

The bartender's countenance changed quickly. "Well, sure. I run a little Italian lottery here myself for the fun of it. I'll pay five hundred times on a straight pick three and eighty-three times on a box."

"Where are the numbers from?" The man kept his eyes on the bartender as he drained a second glass of Pappy.

"Each morning, *The Clarion* lists the handle at the track for the win, place, and show betting from the previous day. The three number picks are the last whole-dollar digits for the three pools." The bartender showed him the newspaper and pointed to the data.

"So, the winning numbers for yesterday are six, eight, and one. Right?"

"Yes, sir, you've got it." The bartender aped a top-notch salesman trying to close the deal.

"Okay, I want a straight pick three with the numbers four, five, and seven. Those were the horses that won me all this money." He raised and lowered his hand full of cash.

"How much do you want to bet?"

"A thousand dollars."

The bartender twisted his neck and moved in closer to whisper, "You do know that the odds are one-thousand-to-one, and if you win, the payoff is only five hundred times the bet?"

"I do. I'm feeling lucky."

The bartender wrote the date, amount, and series of numbers on a blank pre-printed ticket, and then crimped the chit with a seal to authenticate it. He stuck the ticket in the sucker's hand and said, "Good luck."

The man handed over ten hundreds and asked, "When can I pick up my winnings, if my luck holds out?" He appeared mighty sober for someone that had just tossed off two big shots of whiskey.

"Right here at the bar at about seven fifteen tomorrow evening." The man tucked the ticket in his wallet, smiled weakly, and exited with more grace than he demonstrated when he entered. The bartender had paid out only nineteen pick three straight tickets over the last twenty-four years against 20,000 plus in bets. He thought the man to be an utter fool.

OVER FIFTY YEARS AGO

Lissette Carmody and Garth Baldwin were both born on March 10, 1969, the day Led Zeppelin released its first single in Germany, "Good Times Bad Times." Three months earlier, with their first album in the can, the band opened for Vanilla Fudge in Seattle, upstaging them badly, changing the course of music forever.

Garth Baldwin entered this world in a Magoffin County clinic near downtown Salyersville, Kentucky. He played basketball in high school and got his nose smashed in under the basket. The nose never got set, leaving it flat on Garth's face, making him look a little oafish and sinister. He was neither. He graduated valedictorian in his class. Garth went on to learn about coal mining at Transylvania University, which set him up for a successful career at the Stinking Creek Coal Company. Everything was going his way except in the female department. He loved women, but they apparently didn't love him.

Lissette Carmody came from the wrong side of the tracks. Born in Memphis, she was an afterthought for her desultory parents. They took her in stride like everything else in life. Lissette was smart—street smart, that is. She learned how to get by without any help from anybody. When she got pregnant with Bridgett, it was clear that the father would not be coming around.

Things proved hard for Bridgett and her mother until she hit a straight $20 pick three that paid $10,000. Lissette, who preferred Liz, took the money and loaded up a second-hand car with the little child and drove to Kentucky. Her plan was to establish a "numbers" business of her own. She decided the best location for that endeavor would be a sleepy town strategically located at the center of Lexington, Louisville, Cincinnati, and Frankfort, a place called Pleasureville.

Liz rented a two-story brick house near the main intersection of the village and went to work. Her first employee was a local man that used his own car to pick up bets and deliver payouts. Initially, it only took a couple of hours to run the route, but after Liz got the whole network of fifteen betting stations set up, the trip took nearly seven hours.

The locations that accepted the bets got 15 percent, and the payouts ran 50 percent. The rest of the expenses amounted to 10 percent, leaving a 25 percent profit for Liz, which tallied as much as $100,000 a year. At that level, she could build up a cash reserve over time to protect against an extremely lucky player. Bettors used bookies because the tax-free winnings were higher than the legal lottery. If Liz were to miss a payout, she would be out of business, and likely in jail.

Bridgett had grown into a beautiful woman, strawberry blonde, peaches and cream. Her looks came from her tow-headed father, whom she had never seen. Bridgett generally got what she wanted when she gazed at men with those sultry green eyes. She liked flashy men, and they loved her. Liz had the money to put Bridgett through Transy, and did so.

Garth decided to quit Stinking Creek in favor of starting his own coal company. He asked his younger brother, Hophni, to join him. Hophni was broke and sincerely wanted to earn more money, but said no because he loved his job writing sports articles for *The Clarion*.

Absent a partner, Garth forged ahead, buying up coal properties at a rapid clip. Before long, he was stripping land and working mines all over the place. He never took any time off and sorely needed a right-hand man or woman. He called Transy and asked them to set up interviews with recent grads looking for a job. The first interview Garth conducted was with Bridgett Carmody. He hired her on the spot.

TWO YEARS AGO

Garth had visions of a May-December romance involving Bridgett. She never flirted overtly or came on to him, but he felt there was something there. He needed to be sure that she wanted a relationship. While he waited for a signal, his coal company became more complicated and harder to manage.

"Bridgett, we should come up with a way to cut down on absenteeism. I can't seem to get the men to work a full week," Garth complained.

"There's an easy answer to that. Buy them all lottery tickets every day and tell them they must be at work to win."

"But I have about fifty men. How much will that cost me?"

"Fifty dollars a day, twelve or thirteen thousand a year," she calculated.

"Explain it a little better."

"Have the men pick three numbers and write them down on a sheet at the end of their shift. Publish the winning numbers the next morning after they get to work. They'll be curious to find out if they won. Trust me, they'll come streaming in, especially if you have a few winners in a year." Bridgett studied Garth to see if he liked the idea.

"You mean I have to pay for winners too?" He put on a sour face.

"No, you lay that risk off on a bookie, namely my mother."

"She's a bookie? What the hell?" he squawked. Garth rubbed his head with both hands and walked in a circle like he was playing Duck, Duck, Goose. Something didn't add up. Why couldn't he just pay for winners out of the dollar-a-day per man he would fork over to fund the pool? A seed of doubt regarding Bridgett sprouted in his mind. He stopped in his tracks and said, "I guess we can give it a try. Where do we put down the bets?"

"The closest place is Ten Furlongs," she replied.

Absenteeism dropped dramatically within six months. Things were going good in the field due to the betting game. There had only been one $500 lottery winner during that period, but it had been enough to keep hope and enthusiasm alive among the miners. Garth, however, had turned his attention to another problem. His coal company made good money every year, yet he had a nagging suspicion that Bridgett was stealing from him.

It took a long time to find out how the money was being embezzled. Garth discovered the scam purely by accident when he noticed that a check made out to Stuyvesant Trucking had been endorsed by Lissette Carmody. Bridgett had apparently been processing dummy invoices, and then mailing the payments for the phony charges to her mother. Liz must have set up an account at a bank in the name of the trucking company. Garth wasn't quite sure where the money went after being deposited, but he had a hunch Liz wrote checks to cash and stuffed it in her safe or kicked it back to Bridgett. From that point on, Garth personally approved all invoices that were to be paid.

"How's your mother's business going?" Garth asked in a casual manner.

"Good, I think. Seems to be foolproof as far as I can tell." Bridgett sensed that something was wrong.

"No business is foolproof," he replied in an ominous voice.

"Why do you ask?"

"Oh, I just worry about things unnecessarily. It's my nature," he replied in self-deprecating fashion.

TWO WEEKS AGO

Hophni entered the offices of Garth's coal company and introduced himself to Bridgett as he approached her desk. "I'm Garth's brother. What's a nice girl like you doing in a place like this?" he inquired.

Bridgett turned on the charm with her green eyes, and shot back, "Just waiting for handsome men to come by and introduce themselves."

"That leaves me out then." He put on a show of disappointment.

"I'm not so sure about that," she replied in a luscious tone. Hophni shook off the temptation to continue the conversation and sauntered into Garth's office.

After a half-hour meeting, he came out to find Bridgett filing invoices in an alphabetical crib across the room. She turned to face him. He said, "Garth tells me he couldn't run this place without you. I'd ask for a raise if I were you." He walked out without making eye contact. Bridgett simpered and returned to her work.

Bridgett went into Garth's office an hour later, intending to make a clean breast of things. Instead, she asked, "Are you attracted to me?"

"Have been since I first saw you," he answered sheepishly.

"Maybe we can go on an official date sometime."

"Yes. I would like that." Garth knew he couldn't go soft now, this far along.

TWENTY-FOUR HOURS AGO

"What are you doing here so late, Hophni?" asked one of the pressmen.

"Trying to edit an article before the deadline," he responded vacantly.

"You'll have to go straight into the tape if you're going to make any changes now."

"Yeah, I know, I've done it before." He opened up the master tape file and scanned for the information. He changed three numbers, and then moved to the article he had written for publication the next day. Hophni made some minor changes to the piece, and then hit update and save. He shut down his system and left hastily.

FIFTEEN HOURS AGO

Liz poured her first cup of coffee and unfolded a copy of *The Clarion* like she did every morning to see what the winning numbers were for yesterday's lottery. She wrote down four, five, and seven on the ledger and pulled out the sheets from the fifteen betting stations to scan them for winners. She grabbed the paper again to confirm the numbers as panic and dread came over her. There wasn't enough money in the safe to cover the winning bet.

"Bridgett, this is your mother. I've been hit for five hundred thousand, and I only have two hundred forty-one thousand in cash."

"Geez, Mom. How did somebody catch a thousand-dollar ticket?"

"I don't know, but the money has to be in Ten Furlongs at seven this evening, or my goose is cooked."

"Let me see if I can borrow the rest from Garth." She hung up and leaned back in her seat.

After she explained the situation to him, he said, "Your mother will have to sign a note to me, and I will personally deliver the two hundred fifty-nine thousand to Ten Furlongs myself."

"Mom's runner should carry it into the bar to avoid any suspicion," she suggested.

"Alright. I'll meet him in the parking lot and put my money in the briefcase with the rest of it. Then I'll watch him go in."

THREE HOURS AGO

The runner sat in Garth's car, surreptitiously loading the black briefcase with what was needed to make up the balance of the five-hundred-thousand-dollar payout. When he finished packing the cash, he stepped from the car and strolled toward the back door of the bar. He knocked, and the door swung open. The runner stepped inside. He emerged again in ten minutes and reported that everything had gone smoothly.

Inside Ten Furlongs, an attractive woman that had been sitting at the bar for nearly an hour kept asking the bartender trivial questions. "So, when did that Van Winkle whiskey first go in a barrel?"

"Nineteen sixty-eight, I believe."

"What makes it so good?"

"That's a hard question to answer," he commented, hoping the woman would leave it at that. She looked toward the door, stood up abruptly, paid the bill and tip with cash, spoke no more, and moved off in the direction of the ladies room. She carried something that had a raincoat draped over it.

The incredibly lucky man that owned the winning lottery ticket appeared at the bar, pulling the bartender's attention away from the woman. "Hey, what do you have to say about my good fortune?" He smacked his hands down on the bar and crowed like a rooster.

"You're the luckiest man I've ever met."

"Have you got my money ready?" the man asked as he shrugged his shoulders to adjust the beige cotton-twill blazer he had on.

"Here you go," the bartender said. "It's all there, I counted it myself." He handed the briefcase to him around the end of the bar. When the man took the money, his sport coat fell open, exposing a pistol in a holster.

"How about another shot of that expensive whiskey?" the man demanded. "And have one on me," he added. This time he tossed two hundreds up on the bar. For some reason, he didn't seem like the same rube that had placed a bet yesterday. Once he downed his drink, the man shuffled in the direction of the restroom, clutching the briefcase. The bartender saw him step into the women's room by accident and retreat quickly to correct his mistake. He walked straight through the front door a few minutes later, carrying his winnings—high, wide, and handsome.

Hophni brought the briefcase over to Garth's car and said, "I should've joined the Screen Actors Guild. I'll pick up my cut later this week." He nodded pleasantly, got in his own car, and drove off like he was late for another meeting.

The woman, still toting a satchel of some kind under a raincoat, emerged from the ladies room and left Ten Furlongs several minutes after Garth drove away.

ONE HOUR AGO

Garth set the briefcase on the desk and flopped down in his chair with a grimace of exhaustion. Now that he had gotten all of his money back that Bridgett and her mother had stolen, he pondered his romance that had been heating up over the last two weeks. Garth was over fifty and had never been married. He knew that people were wondering if he would ever take a wife. He made up his mind; he was going to marry Bridgett.

Garth opened the briefcase to find hundreds on top and ones underneath. There was roughly $5,000 there in total, not $500,000. He jumped up and ran out to Bridgett's work area. There was nothing personal to be found when he pulled open the desk drawers. She had pulled out. How did the money get switched in the bar? Hophni would know. He tried to call him, but there was no answer. When he arrived at Hophni's house, he saw through the window that the place was completely empty. He had pulled out too.

THE DEALER DOWNSTAIRS

Ella Schleifer and Siegfried Ditsch met forty years ago in a sophomore history class at Western Kentucky University. A romance between them blossomed quickly, and they married in a quiet ceremony seventeen days after graduating from college. Both sets of their Jewish parents that attended the wedding fled to the United States to live with relatives before the Nazis occupied Austria in World War II. Ella studied art, and "Siggi" trained for a career in finance. His first and only offer of employment, which he gleefully accepted, came from a privately owned bank in a sleepy little town in western Kentucky.

Vienna proper was a scant one square mile, off the beaten path. There were 503 citizens in the community at that time, all white people except for the two Native Americans, six Hispanics, and a mixed-race person.

The age-old reputation of Jewish people quickly lifted Siggi's career to a loan officer and bank manager. Knowing that Ella had an artistic eye, Siggi commissioned her to design a dream house for them to be built in a lush grove of trees overlooking the pastoral rolling hills surrounding Vienna.

The three-story edifice, hardly visible from Erzbisch Highway, had a steep peak over the entire right half. Enclosed verdigris-copper porches on the front left corners of the second and third floors contrasted the desert sand and raw umber stucco walls. The white chamfered windows were Dutch in style, along with the slate roof and galvanized chimneys. A capacious three-car detached garage stood off to the side of the house so as not to block the marvelous view out the back.

Siggi and Ella entertained in the home for many years and became friends with most of the educated folks in town, especially the Heinzes and Hofrats. They attended functions with them at the Christian churches from time to time to be sociable. Things went their way until Siggi contracted leukemia. He lived for six more weeks.

Before he died, Siggi consolidated the Ditsch family assets into gold coins because he didn't trust the financial system that he knew so well. Though he hadn't told Ella about it, there was also a growing presence of drug trafficking all over western Kentucky. He knew it was only a matter of time before a character like Kurtz from *Heart of Darkness* arrived in Vienna.

Being practical, the first thing she did after Siggi's death was to divide the house into four apartments. The third floor, with stairs that led down to the back door, was converted into a flat and small area appropriately called the maid's quarters. The second floor and most of the first were the main dwelling. The music room had a small refrigerator, hot plate, bathroom across the hall, and access to the rear entrance of the house for coming and going.

Ella spent most of her time in the music room on the sofa next to the piano. The washed-out walls, unadorned and exposed, soon began to irritate her. She remembered an art store from her college days in Bowling Green that carried provocative, eclectic artwork. A road trip seemed in order to find something to improve the surroundings.

She saw the odd-looking piece hanging high on an interior wall of the overstuffed shop. Her knowledge of Egon Schiele came from a class she had taken in school on modern European art. It was certainly his unmistakable style, a distorted sketch of a pregnant woman. "How did you come by that interesting drawing?" Ella asked the shop proprietor.

"A ninety-seven-year-old man with a thick accent sold it to me. He said his father bought it at an art expo in Austria right after World War One. I gave him a thousand dollars."

"Did he say who the artist was?"

"Said it was somebody that died from the Spanish flu pandemic of nineteen eighteen."

"I like it, and want to buy it," she declared. "Do you have the name of the man who sold it to you?"

He responded, "I do. The sketch is yours for two thousand dollars."

Ella made the purchase, and when she got home, hurriedly mounted it over the piano. The agonizing picture made the atmosphere in the room feel even gloomier. She became more fearful and lonelier with each glance at the sketch, which prompted her to convince an unmarried friend, Olivia Kosmin, to rent the third-floor flat. Ella affectionately referred to her as Aunt Olivia. Their time together softened her sense of isolation and despair when she reminisced about her life with Siggi.

The knock on the door startled Ella. She froze in the kitchen of the main living quarters and felt as though she had been caught slinking around in the wrong part of her own house. She swung open the door to find a shifty-looking brute that had fifteen extra pounds from too much good life. "Are you Ms. Ditsch?" he asked. His expression signaled that he really didn't care if she was or not.

"Yes."

"I heard you have an apartment here I can rent with my girl-friend."

Pretty presumptuous of him, she thought. "I haven't advertised for renters."

He pushed her aside, walked in, and asked, arms akimbo, "Is this it?"

"This is my home." She hoped to rebuff his advance.

"Look, lady, we're setting up shop here, and if you know what's good for you, you'll show me where everything is."

"No," she said.

"Let me make it plain. I'll have you killed if you cause me any trouble. Don't tell anybody anything about anything, and we'll get along just fine. Where will you be staying in the house until we find you a more suitable place to go?"

She shuddered in fear. "There is a music room at the back of the house. What is your name, if I may ask?" Her mind raced after she spoke.

"Herbert Binger," he replied while walking away from her in the direction of the kitchen. He went room to room, swiveled his head around, and opened closets until he found one upstairs that had a freestanding safe in it. "Well now, what have we here? Open it."

"I don't know the combination," she said.

"Open it, or I'll put you in the trunk of my car with tape over your mouth and leave you there until you die."

She begrudgingly obeyed and unlatched the door to expose the stacks of gold coins. "Don't touch those," she implored.

"Right." His eyes got big as he wrung his hands. "Find me a couple of cloth bags to put these in. I'll keep them safe for you." Siggi had purchased the coins for $420 an ounce. They were worth three times that now, over $600,000.

"What about my friend who lives in the third-floor apartment?"

"She can stay there if she minds her own business. Tell her what the score is. If I have any trouble, things won't go well for her. I'll be back in the morning with my girlfriend to move in." He hauled the bags of coins to his car and drove off. Ella immediately rushed upstairs to share the bad news with Aunt Olivia.

Binger and his cheap, airhead gun moll settled in the next day. They only had to bring in a few clothes and bags of groceries. Everything else for them to be comfortable was already there. Binger had Ella explain how things worked in the house over the next few days.

The following week, Binger said to Ella, "Ms. Ditsch, I've found a good place for you to stay for a while. It's in Woodge, Kentucky, about fifty miles from here."

"I don't want to leave this house," she lamented.

"Come on now, you'll like it there. You can come back here after we leave in a few months. You don't need to pack much. You'll get your gold back after this is over. Two of my men will drive you down there in the morning. It's a good place, I promise." She nodded in resignation and returned to her meager digs in the music room.

Later that evening, Ella pulled the sketch off the wall and carried it up to the maid's quarters on the third floor. She used Olivia's phone to call the Heinz family to ask for asylum. Mr. Heinz picked Ella up at two o'clock the next morning, standing in the moonlight out on Erzbisch Highway. At daylight, Binger noticed that she was gone, but quickly got distracted by some sort of business trouble.

Word spread to the Hofrats that Ella was hiding. Since Mr. and Mrs. Heinz both worked, Ella existed alone in the house all day. She dared not go near any windows for fear of being seen. Olivia mailed letters to Ella, addressed to the Heinzes, to stay in touch. One letter declared that she had to sell the sketch in the maid's quarters to the Hofrats to pay expenses.

Ella spent her time hiding in a narrow space behind a large blanket box and the cupboard. She passed the hours playing chess in her mind and practicing Yiddish. She wore only a homemade house dress that was too big and a pair of knit socks. After a few weeks, she became gaunt, pale, and despondent.

One night, two of Binger's goons forced their way into the house. The meaner-looking one asked, "Where are you hiding the Ditsch woman? Turn her over, or we'll turn this place upside down."

Mr. Heinz replied calmly, "Go ahead, she's not here." They proceeded to ransack the place without any success. As they were digging through the closet in the master bedroom, Ella slipped from her hiding place and ran out the front door. She scrambled on foot to the small hospital three blocks up the street.

Heinz tried unsuccessfully to call Aunt Olivia after the goons left. He looked out the window and saw the men staked out in a car up the street. He dared not chase after Ella himself for fear that she would be captured. She was, at that time, hiding in a bathroom stall at the hospital, contemplating her next move.

Aunt Olivia saw where Heinz had tried to reach her, so she called him while driving back from an out-of-town birthday party. He explained the situation and asked her to search for Ella. It was one thirty in the morning when Olivia saw the shadowy figure staggering sock-footed in the ditch next to the road leading out of town. She jumped out and shepherded the delirious woman into the passenger side of her car.

Olivia rolled quietly into her normal parking space at the Ditsch house. The two women, clinging to each other, made their way to the lit porch by the back door. As luck would have it, Binger and his paramour were gone. Ella collapsed on the bed when she entered the third-floor flat. Olivia looked at her in horror and covered her with a heavy blanket to hide the shocking frailty.

Ella never left the third floor during the next few months. She didn't even make a move when Aunt Olivia was gone for fear of being heard. Binger went on trips for days at a time, and routinely, boxes of luxurious merchandise would show up at the front door before he returned. At night, truckers would regularly park in front of the garage and load or unload what was sure to be drugs.

Through the window, Ella saw a pallet of boxes marked *Pappy Van Winkle Bourbon.* Most of the other contraband looked like bales of marijuana, packages of powder, or boxes of pills.

The drug dealer downstairs and his girlfriend came and went on a random schedule. Aunt Olivia brought home cold-cut sandwiches and a newspaper for Ella to read almost every day. When Ella got to the story about the man that had been killed in Paducah, she shut her eyes, gritted her teeth, and made fists that loudly crumpled the paper in her hands. Herbert Binger had been beaten to death.

That night, several trucks came to clear out everything in the garage and a few things from the house. Ella saw Binger's girlfriend throw her clothes into the trunk of his car the next morning, and then speed out to the highway.

When Ella went into the big apartment, she was stunned by the amount of expensive merchandise stacked everywhere. She went back up to the third floor to talk with Aunt Olivia. It felt good to have a normal conversation for the first time in over a year.

Ella spent the next day moving back into the main part of the house. She washed the bed linens and scrubbed the bathroom, bedroom, and kitchen to remove the lingering stench of cheap perfume. All the things laying around that didn't belong to her were neatly stacked in the living room. She then got cleaned up, put on clean clothes, and a little makeup before driving into town to thank the Hofrats and Heinzes.

When she returned home later that afternoon, a trailer was backed up to the front door. Several men were briskly carrying anything out of the house that wasn't nailed down. "Hey, what are you doing?" Ella shrieked.

A Russian-looking man with a Samoyed accent stepped in front of her and said, "We're reclaiming the things stolen from us by that rotten German drug dealer." He trooped back through the door to resume loading the truck.

"But most of those things are mine," Ella petitioned. She ran for her car, and when she tried to open the door, the Russian reappeared to yank the keys out of her hand.

"Sit here and don't move until we're gone," he commanded. Within two hours, the place had been completely stripped, including the third floor. Ella went into the music room where the piano used to be and balled up on the floor in the fetal position.

After three hours of melancholy, Ella gathered herself enough to go through the house to see what was left behind—there was nothing, not even light bulbs, toilet paper, or silverware. She stared for a minute at the empty safe, lost in thoughts of her life with Siggi. Snapping out of her trance, she noticed a little edge of something crammed in behind the safe. It was the corner of one of the cloth bags that she had given Binger for the gold coins. Ella shinnied atop the metal box and saw the two cloth bags wedged against the wall. She dislodged them and sat Indian style in the middle of the bedroom floor to count the coins. They amounted to 80 percent of what had been in the safe before this nightmare saga had begun.

Olivia walked into her completely bare apartment to find Ella Ditsch sleeping face down on the floor. Ella awoke, turned over, and shook the cobwebs from her head. "We've been cleaned out. Fortunately, they missed most of the gold that was once in my safe." She dithered and looked dispirited. "I'm leaving here. Going to get a job and an apartment in Louisville."

"Oh no, Ella," Olivia fulminated.

"Here is fifty thousand in gold. You can stay in the house as long as you like. If you pay the expenses on it and keep it up, I'll split what we get for it when you want me to sell it. I really can't thank you enough for what you've done for me. I'll stay in touch." Ella carried the remaining gold coins to her car and remembered that the Russian had taken the keys. She surveyed the area and found them in the grass twenty feet away. As she drove off, Aunt Olivia waved to her from the third-floor window.

The Hofrats sat in the pecky cypress office of the best auction house in Louisville. The agent assigned to work with them declared, "You know, we'll have to trace the provenance of this piece before we can sell it." He pointed at the sketch of the pregnant woman leaning against the wall next to the desk.

Mr. Hofrat said, "We anticipated that, so we got the name of the man that owned it for many years from a friend of ours."

"Good. I'll run this down."

The auction-house agent had an ecstatic expression on his face when they met again three weeks later. "You're not going to believe this. The artwork is worth a small fortune. Egon Shiele's wife died from the Spanish flu on October 28, 1918. She was six months pregnant. In his delirium after her death, Shiele worked tirelessly on this sketch of her and completed it just before he succumbed to the flu himself three days after her death."

"How much do you think it will bring?" asked Mrs. Hofrat.

"Close to two million," he said.

Mr. Hofrat could only say, "Wow." He turned to his wife. She appeared dazed.

The agent said, "You know, it's customary that Jewish families owning artwork during both world wars be considered for a portion of any profits on a sale, as kind of reparations for their suffering and loss. I'll leave that for you to consider."

Ella found a nice apartment on Bern Street in Louisville. She sold her gold coins for cash and got herself set up pretty well. The best parts of her existence were the two jobs she had at the Seelbach Hotel. During the daytime, she worked at the front desk, and by evening she was the hostess at The Oakroom on the second floor.

A few weeks later, a check came in the mail from the Hofrats for $500,000. Ella smiled when she read the explanation for the money during break time at work. When she manned the front desk again, a slick-looking New Yorker trudged in with his bags and announced what name his reservation was under. As Ella processed his paperwork, the man asked, "Do you know where I can buy a bottle of Pappy Van Winkle bourbon?"

"You might try asking the bartender when he comes in." She looked in the direction of the bar on the north side of the main lobby. "Maybe he can help you." Ella gave him a comforting smile. Oh, to be with people again, she reflected.

Money for Nothing, Drinks for Free

PROLOGUE

Sixty-five three-bottle cases of Pappy Van Winkle twenty-year-old bourbon went missing at the Buffalo Trace Distillery in Frankfort, Kentucky, on October 14, 2013. Known as the "Pappygate" case, it took the police five years to prosecute the ten softball buddies involved in the bootlegging ring. There was great national interest in the story, and Pappy's bourbon just kept on going up in price. Plenty more whiskey had been stolen over the years as it turned out. The batch of 195 purloined bottles that brought the pilfering to light now had a street value of a half million dollars.

DOT AND GEORGE

Dot Mendelson was hit or miss on the fitness front, but that didn't keep her from trying. She occasionally made an evening yoga class when her husband George traveled for work. Otherwise, they had cocktails along with diet-busting snacks and a comfort-food supper. George liked his bourbon. He drank any brand priced under ten dollars a fifth, yet did dream of, among other things, someday owning his own bottle of Pappy Van Winkle.

The Golden Core Yoga Studio was in a small strip center next to a Home Depot in Lexington, Kentucky. A butcher sold fresh meats on one side of the exercise facility while a florist hawked fresh flowers on the other. Both had closed at six. Dot tucked her wallet under the driver's seat, stepped out into the twilight, and locked the car doors with the key fob. She mentally braced herself for the rigorous, hour-long yoga session that lay ahead. Once inside, she tossed her car keys up against the wall and meandered over to a spot facing the instructor.

BIRDY AND STOSH

When it got dark enough, Birdy Gomes slipped out of the passenger side of a car parked away from the door of Home Depot and furtively walked toward the yoga studio. She had on a baseball cap and puffy padding around the midsection with side pockets that made her look pregnant. Five vehicles at the curb, like shoe boxes, were neatly in a row. She checked to see if there was a blinking alarm light on the dash, and if not, peened the glass quickly to break it, and deftly reached under the driver's seat to feel for a wallet. She skipped one car and found nothing in another. It took less than two minutes to yield the spoils of her efforts.

Birdy walked into Home Depot with her head down, and a cap pulled low to defeat the surveillance cameras. The greeter yelled out, "Can I help you find something?"

Birdy said, "Gotta pee. This baby ain't helping none." She sighed and grabbed the phony protuberance with both hands. The greeter looked away, not getting a good look at her face as he pointed in the other direction.

The restroom was empty. Birdy chose not to go in a stall to pull the contents out of each hand purse. She stuffed everything in the pockets of her big belly, crammed the empty wallets into the bottom of the trash bin, and headed for the door. Stanley "Stosh" Gomes, her husband, quietly rolled the car in the direction of the exit to fetch her.

"How much cash you get?" Stosh asked.

"Three hundred and five dollars."

"Shoot, that ain't much," he spat, gripping the steering wheel tighter. "What else?"

Birdy riffled through the wad in her hand as though she were culling junk mail. "Several credit cards, three driver's licenses, and some blank checks for a Dorothy Mendelson." She looked at the picture on Dot's license and chirped, "Hey, we could be twins." She showed the photo to Stosh, who seemed disinterested. "The checks are from the bank my sister works at." Stosh wriggled in the seat as an idea was forming in his larcenous mind.

Dot rang her husband to tell him of the misfortune before springing into action. She called each of the credit card companies and contacted the bank, leaving a message for them to watch her money. The following morning she went into the branch where they talked her out of closing the account and into buying a theft protection plan. The police conjectured that the unidentifiable woman on the Home Depot video was probably the culprit. They were frank with Dot. The chances were virtually zero of catching the thief. That motivated her to buy a new wallet on the way to getting a replacement driver's license. The last thing was to get the window glass replaced. Everything would be back to normal when George got home from his sales trip.

GERTY AND BAX

Birdy's sister Gertrude married Baxter Connelly a dozen years ago. An epic mistake. He was a bitter, negative, supercilious man that had given up on his ship coming in. He did the same thing every day—hot shot deliveries of parts, paint, and supplies to auto repair shops that were on a milk run around central Kentucky. He made terrible money with no prospects of doing any better.

Stosh and Birdy left the home rule-class city of Hazard shortly after getting married. The Feds were about to nab Stosh for growing marijuana, so he needed to get off the grid. Since he had never signed any government forms, including a tax return, except for a driver's license application, it was easy for him to just disappear. They wanted to move near Lexington because Gertrude and Baxter lived there. Birdy found a perfect spot for them, a farmhouse rental hidden in a grove of trees at the back of a worn-out horse farm on the line of Fayette and Bourbon counties, owned by a Saudi Arabian who told them when and where to drop the rent money off, in cash.

The farmhouse was built around 1900. Plumbing, heating, and electricity were added in the fifties, and beyond that, the place had been deteriorating ever since. It had a good kitchen, bathroom, living room, and giant-screen satellite television. The smokehouse on the backside of the screened porch was the best feature of the property. It had no windows. The walls were three feet of sawdust, which kept the inside temperature at sixty degrees. The reinforced metal door had fortified hinges, a hardened-steel hasp, and huge padlock.

"Birdy, why don't you see if Bax and Gerty will meet us at Columbia Steak House on Saturday night? Tell 'em I'm buying, drinks and all."

When Gertrude told Baxter about accepting the invitation, he whimpered. He hated Stosh with a passion. The man never worked. All he did was play softball and talk about his "marvelous" gun collection that he kept locked up in the smokehouse. The worst thing was that Stosh lent Baxter $500 when Baxter was in a pinch, which had not been paid back yet. Stosh always had money. Where in the hell did he get it?

Birdy greeted Gertrude with, "Hi there, Gerty. Good to see you again."

Gertrude was as nice as Baxter was sour. "You're looking well. Wonderful to see you," she offered, giving Birdy a warm, loving hug.

Stosh presented a hand to Baxter and said, "Hello, fella, and to you, Miss Gertrude. Bartender, bring us a couple of Pappys on the rocks, and some Chardonnay for the ladies. Thanks." There he goes again, Baxter thought, throwing money around.

While they waited for the steaks to come, Stosh admitted obsequiously, "Gerty, I need your help. I just sold some guns to a guy, and his wife paid me with a personal check from your bank. I don't want to try to cash it until I know there is enough in the account for it to clear. Also, if you could get me a copy of her signature, I can make sure there won't be a problem with that."

"What would you like me to do?" Gertrude asked in a soft tone.

"First, get me what her signature looks like, and second, eyeball her account balance at three o'clock every Friday until we catch it above twenty thousand. The check I'm holding is just under that." Stosh was a better liar than truth teller. "Oh, and let's forget about the five hundred that Bax owes me. We're all good." Baxter's blood pressure rose 50 percent.

"I see no harm in that. Now, how's everything else with you guys?"

Birdy wagged her head and replied, "Mighty good, I guess. Stosh has been making a little money trading guns. How about you folks?"

The word "bullcrap" popped into Baxter's mind, but instead, he stated, "Same old sixes and sevens."

The steaks were good as usual. The girls made pleasant small talk, and the men fell silent. On the way out, Stosh gave final instructions. "Call Birdy's cell phone a little after three on Friday. I don't want to run into any hassle getting my money. Thanks,

Gerty." Stosh gave her a little hug, which he had never done before. Baxter contemplated hugging Birdy, then instantly felt repulsed by the idea.

George Mendelson got his sales commission check once a year. With a Red Skelton grin on his face, he put it in Dot's hot little hand. "Almost twenty-four thousand, what do you say to that?" he asked rhetorically. George strutted over to the liquor bar like Baby Huey to pour himself two fingers of eight-dollar bourbon. The taste of it reminded him of why he drank Manhattans. Since Dot ran the finances in the house, she would put the money into checking, clean up all the bills, and move the rest of it into the savings account early next week.

Incredibly, the first Friday call that Birdy got from Gertrude was in the affirmative, nearly a balance of $25,000. Stosh heard the conversation and leaped out of his chair. "Let's go," he said as he tucked Dot's license and the bogus check made out to Dorothy Mendelson in his shirt pocket. Stosh had replaced the license plate on their car with a stolen one. As they sped off together to the bank, he told Birdy, "Make relaxed small talk and laugh a little when they can hear you." She bobbed her head in response.

MONEY FOR NOTHING

Birdy wheeled into the drive-through and rolled down the window. She said, "I want to cash this." She placed the license and dead check for $3,000 in the vacuum tube. The teller reviewed Dorothy Mendelson's balance, seeing it was adequate to cover the amount due. The theft alert that Dot bought, because of an administrative snafu, had not been activated. Birdy and Stosh were prepared to pull away if there was any trouble, but instead, the money and Dot's license plopped down, right within arm's reach. Birdy deliberately retrieved the packet and drove away slowly.

When back on the main road, Stosh bellowed, "Yes! Call Gerty and tell her we're going to Cincinnati tomorrow to cash the check and blow off a little steam. If there is anything wrong, she will mention it to you. If not, we're in the clear. She won't suspect that the three thousand is related to us."

Gertrude told Baxter about the call and trip to Cincinnati that Stosh and Birdy had planned for Saturday. Baxter surreptitiously went out to the garage after supper to find the bolt cutters. He put them in the bed of his pickup truck that had a tonneau cover on it to protect the contents from theft and rain. Gertrude sensed something was different. Baxter was actually gentle and pleasant to her the rest of the evening, totally out of character.

Stosh and Birdy made out several of Dot's checks to *Cash*. Birdy had practiced the signature many times before using it. They also identified where the bank branches were in Cincinnati, and the route they would take. After crossing the Ohio River, Stosh said to Birdy, who was driving, "I like this town." He acted just like a two-bit grifter. Birdy looked a little harder with each passing year.

Baxter crunched the gravel driveway with his truck tires as he drove up to the Gomes farmhouse. The wind didn't blow, and sun didn't shine—perfect weather for what he had in mind. He grabbed the bolt cutters and peered at the massive padlock on the smokehouse door. He dropped the cutters and went into the house through the unlocked backdoor. Baxter spent fifteen minutes looking for the padlock key. Found it under the throw rug in the bedroom.

Birdy and Stosh approached the first drive-through at nine o'clock. She presented the check made out to *Cash* for $3,000 and Dot's license. The teller sent back thirty hundreds without as much as a "do-si-do" or "how do you do." They hit five more branches, one every thirty minutes, ending up with $18,000. Stosh knew better than to push his luck and chance overdrawing the account.

Halfway back to Lexington, Stosh changed out the license plates behind a gas station. He threw Dot's driver's license, checks, and the stolen plate into a retention pond that was nearby. It was almost one o'clock, time for lunch.

Baxter had to make a lot of runs between the smokehouse and his truck. He engaged the padlock again and threw the key into the woods as far as he could. The pickup rode too low on the way out, scraping the gravel driveway in several spots. He disappeared over the hill about three seconds before Stosh and Birdy came barreling toward the farm entrance from the other direction.

Stosh ordered Birdy to put the cash in the smokehouse. "The key isn't under the rug," she replied.

"Well, where is it?"

"If I knew, I wouldn't have asked." She glared at him, hands on her hips.

"I'll deal with that when I need something out of there. Maybe we'll find the key by then."

On Monday morning, Dot went online to move $20,000 to the savings account. It took her a few minutes to figure out that she had been hit for $21,000, a cashed check that bounced, and six separate cash withdrawals. She went to the branch, demanding reimbursement for the loss, got it, closed her accounts, and walked next door to start doing business with a national bank.

Baxter paid the rent on an air-conditioned storage unit a year in advance out of some cash that he had found in the Gomes smokehouse. He unloaded everything in about twenty minutes. As he was heading home, he felt a bliss that magically transformed his personality. His ship, in fact, had come in. He would act like it now. The first such gesture was the pleasant smile he flashed at Gertrude before giving her a heartfelt kiss.

Three days later, Baxter began to wonder why Birdy hadn't called Gertrude to report the guns being missing. He grew increasingly paranoid. What if Stosh suspected him of the theft? Could he be following him or setting a trap? Baxter had to do something, go on the offensive. He came up with a diabolical plan that might work.

That evening, Gertrude was in tears. She confessed, "They suspect me of being involved in the Mendelson theft. I might get fired if they get enough evidence." Her sobbing began ratcheting up.

"Don't worry about it, honey. We don't need the money right now." Baxter tried futilely to soothe her. She didn't know exactly what he meant and didn't feel like pursuing it.

Stosh finally cut the lock off the smokehouse door to find it completely empty. He surmised that it had been cleaned out by somebody on his softball team. They all knew what was in there. Nobody else did. He jumped in his car, intending to interrogate them, one by one. He didn't even have a gun to use for persuasion. The tires spun, and gravel flew as Stosh shot out to the paved road. In his line of "work," these things happened. The percentages were high that his cache was long gone.

Baxter found a blank card and wrote out a personal note.

Dear Dorothy,

Please accept this gift as a token of my appreciation for letting me clean out your bank account.

Sincerely,

> *Stanley Gomes*
> *Hazard, Kentucky*

"Gerty, where does that Dorothy Mendelson live?"

She looked at him and didn't speak right off. Her eyes were puffy and red. "The address on her check was eight seventeen Charmaine Court. Why do you want to know?"

"Just curious. Wonder if she's married? The checking account was just in her name, right?"

"Yes, I think she is," Gertrude replied.

"I should have known Stosh was conning you. He's a bad apple. Do you think Birdy knows that?"

"Be hard not to, wouldn't it?"

Baxter declared, "If you go down for this, I'm not going to stand for them getting away with it."

"What are you going to do about it?"

"Not sure yet," he said as he stood up to walk out of the room. Baxter grabbed the note he wrote, climbed into his truck, and drove to the storage unit.

DRINKS FOR FREE

Charmaine Court was a good fifteen miles from where Baxter had his stash. It took him no more than twenty-five minutes to get there in light traffic. The street was dark enough so that he could place the package and note on the front porch without being seen. He reckoned that Dorothy would call the police. They would start searching for Stosh in Hazard. Eventually, there'd be an APB out for him, and he would have to leave Kentucky.

Dot saw the package and note the next morning when she retrieved the newspaper, but did not show it to George. After he went to work, she studied the box and read the note several times before shredding it and throwing it in the garbage. She wasn't out any money and didn't want any hassle from the police, and besides, the box had intrinsic family value.

When George got home that evening, Dot presented the wrapped package to him, and said, "Open it."

He ripped into it immediately and blurted, "Pappy Van Winkle twenty-year-old. Is it for me?"

"Of course," she replied with the happiest of grins.

George went to the bar, opened one of the three bottles, poured a dram, and took a sip. Life was beyond good at that moment and would be for as long as the whiskey held out.

THE HEN WITH THE SAPPHIRE PENDANT

Gordon Treacher had no intention of toiling away for fifty years to get rich. He finished high school in 1964, and shortly thereafter, married the love of his short life, Emily Dolan. She nearly always supported his get-rich-quick schemes and anything else he said or did. The best easy-money plan he had come up with was buying stuff at auctions and estate sales that he could flip to furniture, art, coin, jewelry, and firearms dealers for a quick profit.

The first estate sale Gordon set his sights on had a listing of 109 entries. When the auction began, eagerness showed in his bidding, but soon he became disillusioned when each entry sold for a price much higher than he was willing to pay. Somewhat despondently, he pursued a cheap necklace long enough to get it. Near the end of the auction, he kept raising his hand in desperation, trying to win anything, like the little sparkly knickknack that was now being offered. How would he justify paying $3,000 for it to Emily?

When a jeweler that Gordon trusted looked at the pieces, he quickly dismissed the jewelry as worthless and assiduously studied the knickknack for what seemed like fifteen minutes. He finally looked up, and in a trance-like manner, said, "You will never have to work another day in your life. This maker's mark is authentic. Do you want to sell it?"

"How much is it worth?"

The jeweler reached for a book on the shelf behind him, found the page with the sketch, spun it around, and pointed at the description. "In the millions. It should keep going up in value."

"I think I'll just take a loan out on it and live like a king," Gordon proposed.

"You can borrow against this thing for the rest of your life," he said. "Don't drop it."

Once the bauble was confidentially appraised, the bank insisted on keeping it in their safe as security for the loan. Gordon walked out with a big check and then sent a small one to his jeweler friend as a thank-you.

The Treachers decided to purchase a well-maintained thorough-bred horse farm in Kentucky with their newfound wealth. They renamed the place Sapphire Stud and quickly learned that the horse business was for rich people that cared more about status than cash flow. Nonetheless, they started rubbing elbows with the local gentry. Life was good, except for one thing. There were no children around.

Gordon and Emily had been trying, without success, to have a baby for ten years. As hope waned, they applied with an adoption agency and were approved for the placement of a child. Just after they received the news, Emily got pregnant, naturally. Lucas was born in the winter of 1975. There were so many complications during his birth that she lost the ability to bear children anymore. That motivated the Treachers to tell the adoption agency how they would really like a girl, which is what they eventually got.

Xenia Dagmar, a two-year-old Russian girl, arrived in early 1977. Coincidentally, the birth date of their son Lucas fell three days after Xenia's. Since the children were the same age, it made no sense for Zeeny, as she was called, to take the Treacher name.

The kids grew up together as good friends. Gordon and Emily refused to spoil them. In fact, they went out of their way to make sure the children earned what they got. Zeeny and Luke became resentful. Scions of other horsemen were given anything they wanted.

Xenia and Lucas graduated from high school together in 1993. Neither had an interest in college, so they worked the farm alongside the hired help—Todd Shively, Joel Fromstein, and Octavius Ford. Zeeny lamented, "I wish I had the money to buy a place. I want to be on my own." She had come face-to-face with the harsh reality of the prospects of life in the Treacher family. Gordon, as she called him instead of Dad, did not part with money easily.

Luke replied, "Someday. Come on, let's turn these horses out for the night."

On Tuesday, November 30 of that same year, three brazen men robbed a Brinks truck in broad daylight at a branch bank in Cincinnati. Two of the men zoomed up in a stolen white minivan, left it running, jumped out, fired a dozen warning shots, and took two of the three bags of cash that were on a cart near the back of the truck. A third man picked up the thieves in a stolen silver Jeep. They sped off together to a nearby nursing home parking lot, where a fourth person waited for them in another getaway vehicle. They vanished, not seen or heard from since. It was the first Brinks pickup at that location after the "Black Friday" shopping weekend, which meant the robbery had been well planned and executed. The take was $500,000.

Right after Christmas, heading into the busiest season for a horse farm, the three longtime hands abruptly quit. To make things worse, Zeeny had scraped together enough money to buy a small farm of her own. The Treachers were left short-handed. They had a difficult time finding good help to replace Todd, Joel, and Octavius.

It was just a matter of weeks before the newspaper reported that Octavius Ford had been killed near his home by a hit-and-run driver.

Xenia Dagmar's fledgling farm, named Hermitage Stud, began to prosper within a couple of years. She walked away from the barn, exhausted after a long day with the horses, and saw a familiar truck coming up the driveway. It was Todd Shively. "Hi there, Zeeny," he said. "How are you? Beautiful as ever I see." He approached her wearing an apprehensive expression and the same old boots she had ever seen him in.

"Doing fine, Todd. It really hurt us when you left."

He responded with, "Didn't mean any harm. Just needed a break. Would you be able to hire me back?" Might as well lay it right out there. He had known Zeeny since she was a kid.

"Sure. Heard anything from Joel?"

"He's back with the Treachers," Todd reported.

"That's interesting. Same wages you left us at?"

"Why not. I can prove myself again. Maybe you'll pay me more later." He was relieved that she seemed so receptive.

She thought that last comment sounded like blackmail. "Did you hear about Octavius?"

"Went to his funeral. Damn drunk drivers."

"Will I see you in the morning at six?" she asked.

"Never been late yet." He doffed his cowboy hat and threw it on the seat of his pickup. She watched as he pulled away, wondering if he had tried to get back on at Sapphire too.

The sweltering summer day finally broke into wind and rain that had turned fierce, prompting Todd to take shelter in the barn along with the horses. When Zeeny noticed that his truck was still there after four o'clock, she went to check things out. Tree branches were strewn all over the wet yard. She reattached the barn ground wire that was loose, and saw Todd up against a stall, slumped over like a man taking a siesta. He was dead. It was determined to be an accidental electrocution.

When Gordon Treacher heard about Todd's death, he got nervous and suspicious. He hired a private investigator to find out about Xenia's family background in Russia. When he read the report that came in three months later, one of the schemes that he was famous for came into his head. He called his longtime jeweler friend in Chicago, who was by then past retirement age. Gordon told him what he wanted done. The jeweler's son was an even better craftsman than his father. He lit up when he heard about the order.

In the fall of 1997, Lucas came running into the house. He yelled for his dad, who emerged from the study. "What is it?"

Out of breath, Luke choked out, "Something bad has happened to Joel."

"What?" Gordon asked impatiently.

"Come see." Lucas flailed out of the house, and his dad loped closely behind.

Joel Fromstein's neck was at an odd angle. It looked as though he had fallen out of the hayloft onto his head. Gordon surveyed the surroundings quickly. "Has Zeeny been here today?" he asked.

"Yeah, she came by to borrow cotter pins for the mower wheels."

"When was that?"

"She left just before I saw Joel."

"I'll call the police." Gordon stomped toward the house at a brisk pace.

There was no evidence of foul play. Joel Fromstein's death got written up and reported as an accidental fall.

On New Year's, Xenia Dagmar watched football and nursed a slight hangover that she got from drinking too much champagne the night before at a horse-people's party. A knock on the door made her jump up and see who was there. A Slavic man stood on the stoop in a taupe trench coat, feet splayed, hands in his pockets. "Yes?" she quizzed.

"May I come in?"

"What's this about?"

"I have some information about your family in Russia." He leaned his head forward and rolled his eyes upward. She waved him in, moving closer to the pistol that was on the end table. Zeeny told him to sit as she did so herself, next to the gun. "I'm sure you don't remember anything about your homeland. You were only two."

"That's right," she affirmed.

"We have been waiting a long time to make contact. You were placed in this family for a reason." He shrugged his shoulders and bowed his neck.

"Oh, really? Why would that be?"

"You are the great-great-great-granddaughter of Marie Feodorovna," he answered.

"I have no idea who that is." Zeeny waited patiently for the conversation to go somewhere.

"She was Tsarina of Russia before the Revolution."

"I hope you brought me an inheritance check." She suddenly felt the urge to needle him. "I'm American now, not Russian. The only aristocrats I care about are the ones that buy my horses."

"Ah, but there is a way you can be rewarded for your work." He shared many details of the situation with her, then left a phone number that she could call at the appropriate time. After he left,

Xenia, lost in the background noise of the football game on television, pondered what she had heard. Lucas would have to be told.

Gordon paid off the loan on his trove after nearly thirty years. The problem was he had to retake possession of it. He had a massive walk-in safe built at the farmhouse to safeguard it against would-be thieves. A Brinks truck was hired to deliver it safely, with little fanfare. The Treachers could at least trot it out to admire occasionally, or maybe they would sell it.

Gordon and Emily were both over fifty years old now. They had planned an extravagant Easter brunch for Luke and Zeeny. The kids didn't know it yet, but the subject of conversation would be marriage and grandchildren. After all, twenty years old was the right age to get hitched and start having kids. The Treachers intended to bribe them.

When everybody was seated in the dining room, Gordon asked, "Did you notice the centerpiece on the table?"

"We did," Lucas answered. "What is it?"

"The thing that's paid the freight around here. I bought it at an auction years ago. It's worth millions."

"You're kidding," Xenia said with phony awe. "How?"

"It's an Imperial Egg made in eighteen eighty-six by Carl Faberge. Tsar Alexander the Third began giving one of those to his wife, Marie Feodorovna, each year as an Easter gift. This was the second one made and is considered lost or to be in a private collection." A bigger egg opened to reveal a hen in a basket picking an egg out of a nest. The golden hen and basket were studded with rose-colored diamonds. The surprise that came with each Faberge creation was the cabochon-sapphire pendant in the shape of an egg that was held loosely in the hen's mouth.

"It is beautiful," Luke commented. "What are you going to do with it?"

Emily smiled demurely, and then said, "We thought if you kids found soulmates, got married, and started families, we might sell it and invest in bigger farms for each of you."

Lucas grinned and said, "Sign me up for that. All I have to do is find a beautiful horsewoman that will put up with me."

"You're not such a bad catch, Luke, especially if a girl knows you have a grubstake," Zeeny commented, playing with him a little.

Gordon interrupted, "And you, Zeeny, can have any man up and down farm row. Mother and I would like to be young enough to enjoy some grandchildren."

After brunch, Xenia pulled Lucas aside for a private conversation. "Luke, we need to steal that thing and sell it. Some guy from Russia came to see me and offered to buy it for two million dollars."

"Two million, hell, the way he's talking it might be worth ten or twenty million, maybe more. I don't think anybody knows he's got it other than the bank and your Russian guy. Let me find out what a private collector will pay, then you can tell the Russian how much it will cost him."

Zeeny asked, "How are we going to get it?"

"I found the combination to the safe the first week he had it installed. He stuck a piece of masking tape with the numbers on it to the underside of his desk where the drawer pulls out. I tried it; it works."

"He'll know we took it."

"Not if we stage it as a robbery," he retorted.

Two weeks later, Lucas dropped by at sun up to see Xenia. She was in the barn, feeding the horses. "Hello, little brother. It must be something important."

"Money's always important. I found a collector that will pay twenty million for the egg. You can see if your Russian buddy wants to beat that offer."

"I'm not going to call him until we have it. What's your plan for stealing it?" she asked.

"Simple, when they are both out of the house, I'll open the safe, take the egg, leave it open, and be the one to alert Dad. I'll tell him I found it that way, and that someone must have broken in."

"Well, get on with it then." Her tone was like a hangman giving the order to drop the bottom out.

As the days went by, Zeeny began to worry that something had gone wrong. Finally, Lucas called and said, "I can't get the safe open. The combination doesn't work anymore. He must have had it changed."

"Now, what do we do?" She was perturbed.

"I guess I'll try to find out where he has the new numbers hidden," he said.

Gordon showed up at Hermitage Stud several days later, and asked, "What have you done with it?"

"With what?"

"The egg. It's not in the safe," he reported.

"I didn't steal it. Cross my heart, on a stack of bibles, and I promise that I did not take your egg."

"Well, I'm sure Lucas wouldn't have taken it. I'm not sure I believe you." He left in a huff. As soon as Gordon was gone, Zeeny called Luke and told him to come over after work.

"So, what kind of stunt are you pulling?" she demanded.

"Nothing. What do you mean?"

"I can always tell when you are lying."

He exhaled and looked out the window. "I sold it for twenty million to a private collector. I intended to follow through with our plan, but when I got in there, there were two eggs. One was in a box with the paid-off loan papers, so I figured the other one had to be a copy. They looked identical. There's no way a buyer could tell a fake. I took the copy and left the real thing. That way, Dad would not be able to report the loss, and I would be in the clear."

"You mean *we*, don't you?" she corrected him. "I want half."

"Now, wait a minute, Zeeny," he whined.

"Look, Lucas, I know you've killed three people, and were the mastermind behind that bank robbery in Cincinnati. You didn't want anybody around that could turn you in, so you got rid of them. I don't believe you'll kill me."

"How do you think I got the hundred thousand I lent you to buy this farm?"

"That's what put everything together for me. It had to have been ill-gotten gain."

He said, "The money is in cash. I couldn't put it in the bank, and the buyer didn't want there to be a trail. I'll have to bring it over in suitcases. Better find a good place to hide it."

Zeeny called the Russian and told him that she couldn't get the egg because it was in an impenetrable safe. She suggested that he discreetly contact Gordon and make an offer for it himself. The Russian admitted that he had tried to go through her because he thought he could get it cheaper.

Twenty years later, Xenia Dagmar Hancock was married and had three teenage boys. The farm was over 2,000 acres now, and the Romanov dynasty lived on in America. Lucas had been in jail for a few years already for various crimes. He never married. Gordon had recently died of cancer, and it looked like the Treacher line was going to die out.

A FedEx box showed up at the Hancock farm addressed to Xenia. Inside was a bottle of twenty-three-year-old Pappy Van Winkle bourbon, two cashier's checks for $10 million each, and a note from her deceased adopted father.

Zeeny,

I sold the egg to the Russian. Here is your half, and the other half is for Lucas when he gets out of jail. See that he gets it. Enjoy that bourbon on me.

Your father, Gordon

THE HAUNTED HOUSE
OF EDWARD HOPPER

On an early July afternoon in 1980, a salty breeze gusted through downtown Rockland instead of out to sea as it typically did on a Maine summer day. The freight door at the Farnsworth Art Museum remained closed to keep out the humid air. The Whitney Museum in New York was patiently waiting for a packed up watercolor that sat on the workshop floor at the Farnsworth, but since the little crate had no shipping label, straightaway it became a logistical orphan.

The Whitney owned a fifth of the 800-plus works of art by Edward Hopper and had arranged to borrow the 1926 piece acquired by the Farnsworth Museum in 1971, a three-quarter view of a home in Rockland's south end razed by fire years ago. Merely fourteen inches high by twenty inches wide, the watercolor looked crude and sloppy at first glance, morose and quite brilliantly done when studied more carefully.

The Old Boarding House was a tricolor overlay of cadet gray, cobalt blue, and cinnamon brown. Slender chimneys and tent-top dormers stood guard over three floors of boarders, imagined and unseen. True to form for Hopper—lonely, isolated, and sparse. The spectral watercolor was now something else: missing, lost, or stolen.

Police were called in. They concluded that the painting had to be somewhere on the premises. Every square inch of the museum compound got searched again and again, to no avail. The FBI heard rumors that a watercolor fitting the description had been offered for sale in the art underworld. No one could say for sure if it was the real thing.

John Cole, an exhibit technician at the Farnsworth, skittered down the basement steps in late April 1983 to look for crates that could be commandeered for service. In a dark corner, he found one marked *The Old Boarding House.* Museum director, Marius Peladeau, reported that the painting had been readied for shipment nearly three years ago and was undamaged. Checked for authenticity by IFAR, it went back on display under a new name, *The Haunted House,* when the museum reopened the following Tuesday.

Miles Heymark operated an art business out of a regal storefront on Louisville's Whiskey Row. His modus operandi had been to move to a new city every five years to peddle watercolors to a fresh set of customers. Several baize panels dotted with framed art were visible through the street-side windows. Gimcrack here and there made the place look deceptively sophisticated. Behind the wall in the back were painting supplies, his expensive camera, and an old-style fire safe that had been dragged around from place to place.

Miles just turned sixty years old and still had a proud, patrician face that was topped with wavy blond hair. He dressed for business that day in a blue button-down shirt and gray tweed sport coat. Pleated navy slacks broke fashionably over his polished black brogans.

At closing time, Miles locked up and scooted over to the Kentucky Center to hear the orchestra. Once seated, he studied the new cellist for more than a minute before a wry grin formed on his face. She was older, had a Greek figure, and face like Nefertiti, only better.

Tina Rand won a seat with the Louisville Orchestra a month ago. She left another city behind to come to Kentucky for a couple of reasons, one being to escape a man obsessed with marrying her. It had been a pattern, sending the wrong signals to men. Women as stunning as her generally kept their distance. Tina, however, loved to talk. While vigorously bowing the cello, she glimpsed the man in the crowd that she had been looking for, and judging by his attire, speculated he would be at the after-party.

Hair of the Wildcat easily handled the throng of people that routinely flooded in when the Kentucky Center let out. Musicians and sycophants frequented the trendy watering hole to unwind after a performance. Miles started going to the parties when he first got to town, and this was Tina's shakedown cruise. He spotted her and sidled up, intending to introduce himself. She turned away, then swiveled around to say, "Were you at the concert?"

"I was, delightful." He stalled under the weight of her comely stare. She was incredibly good-looking. "Miles Heymark is my name."

"Tina Rand. I love your tweed jacket, very smart." Her outfit resembled a matador's uniform, custom fitted, mostly black with garnet accents. Her hair was a caramel swirl falling a foot below the shoulders.

"Thanks. Can I get you something to drink?" he asked.

"A glass of their best Pinot Noir." Miles returned in a few minutes with a wine in one hand and neat Pappy Van Winkle bourbon in the other. "You married?" Tina queried while hiking herself onto the wooden bar chair.

He followed her lead and sat down. "No, never have been."

"Me neither. I've had chances. This is a new town for me now."

"Me too; I opened an art store right up the street."

"What kind of stuff do you have?"

"Watercolors," he said.

"Your work or other artists?"

"Both, but I think my stuff is pretty good," he bragged. "Been doing it a long time."

She flashed a superficial grin, goggled at him, and said, "Sort of like me and the cello."

"I wish I had some musical talent," he replied while shaking a leg to free a pant cuff.

She placed an elbow on the cocktail table and cupped her hand under her chin. Looking him in the eye, she asked, "Know any good restaurants in this town? You could ask me to dinner, you know."

Miles was wondering if she had become a hooker with a website and everything. He hoped not. "What kind of food do you like?"

"Ethnic." She straightened up and daintily sipped her wine.

He thought of a spot that sold his paintings. "Taberna el Norte on Bardstown Road. Tomorrow at seven? Can I pick you up?"

Tina finished her wine, stood up, adjusted her outfit, and strolled over to a half-circle of lecherous violinists. She called out over her shoulder, "I'll meet you there." By his calculation of her age, she must have found the fountain of youth.

Bardstown Road embodied Louisville's avant-garde scene. Taberna el Norte, in the heart of the action, was a Spanish eatery shoehorned into a refitted house. The tessellated tile floor of gray and brown looked cheesy. Sidewalls of brick had rows of artwork for sale. Patrons walked to the back of the place to get seated. The hostess roosted on a low rostrum while the kitchen doors fanned noisily on either side of her as waiters went in and out.

Miles parked his car on Bonnycastle Avenue, facing Bardstown Road. He was wearing blue jeans, buckskin loafers, and a pearwood cashmere sweater with a crew neck. When he entered the restaurant, Tina waved him over to the best table in the house. Her hair was in a ponytail, and she had on a tan suede jacket, skinny black trousers, and Casa Fagliano boots. "This is an interesting place," she allowed.

"Food's good." The waiter came with menus and took their order for a bottle of wine.

"So, what shall we talk about?" she asked.

"Eleanor Roosevelt said that great minds discuss ideas, average minds discuss events, and small minds discuss people. What shall it be?"

She didn't hesitate. "Let's name the top five people in certain areas of art, music, and books. Since you know so much about art, who are the best Italian Renaissance painters?" She hunkered down, leaned forward, and crossed her arms on the table.

"Who said I know that much about art? I say da Vinci, Raphael, Michelangelo, Titian, and Caravaggio." Not a controversial group in his mind.

"I'll take your word for it." The waiter brought the best Pinot Noir in the house and wrote down their dinner orders.

Miles offered a toast and proceeded to ask, "Okay, since you know so much about music, what are the noteworthy recorded songs by American artists between, say, nineteen-fifty and nineteen-seventy?"

"Oh, come on, Miles, there is no right answer to that," she complained. "Who said I know that much about music? There are plenty of examples of great singers and players covering great songwriters and arrangers. All have bodies of work that confirm their greatness, sort of like going undefeated to get in the college football playoffs."

Man, she talked a lot, he thought. "I'm with you so far."

"'Blue Moon of Kentucky' by Elvis Presley, 'I've Got You Under My Skin' by Frank Sinatra, 'Summertime' by Louis Armstrong and Ella Fitzgerald, 'God Only Knows' by the Beach Boys, and 'All Along the Watchtower' by Jimi Hendrix. Shall I explain?"

"Sure," he muttered as the waiter brought food. "I'm interested." Tina went on to tell stories of Bill Monroe, Sam Phillips, Cole Porter, Nelson Riddle, George Gershwin, Tony Asher, Brian and Carl Wilson, and Bob Dylan. She talked incessantly for fifteen minutes, occasionally pausing for a bite of her meal. "Which one is the best?" he asked.

"'Skin.' That crescendo has as much sex in it as a grape has juice. Frank did twenty-two takes." Tina ordered coffee and concluded, "The food was spectacular." She wiped her lips and toweled her hands with fragrant lemon water. "All right, name the best modern American painters of the early to mid-twentieth century."

"Georgia O'Keefe, Thomas Hart Benton, Edward Hopper, Jackson Pollock, and Mark Rothko," he stated.

Tina added, "Rothko reminds me of a fifties, low-budget science-fiction movie. Corny, but you can't stop watching it." She demurred and said, "Do you mean Hopper like that watercolor over there on the wall?" She pointed at *The Old Boarding House* without looking up. "I bought it for eight hundred and fifty bucks before you got here. Pretty steep, I thought," she caviled at the cost. "Wonder who painted it?"

Miles stiffened and looked down at the floor before saying, "I did. Trust me—you got the deal of a lifetime."

"What are you, an art forger?" She smiled like the cat that ate the canary.

He ignored the question and said, "Why don't you come by my shop, and we can talk about it."

"I will." They finished up, Miles paid the bill, and Tina had the hostess bring the painting to her. "Thanks for dinner," she said with a warm smile.

The Kentucky air was clear, sky cloudless, and sun radiant. Miles usually painted from nine until eleven and only went out front if a customer came in. The shop was busy with browsers over the lunch hour when the weather was good. As midday approached, he positioned himself among the merchandise to accost interested lookers.

The shop had emptied by midafternoon. That's when Tina walked in and popped the question. "What are the five bees of Kentucky?" She had on black heels and slacks with a fabric bow-tie belt. The bodice was pewter and white paisley. She wore no makeup and needed none.

Miles looked smug. He said, "There are six. Bourbon, basketball, bluegrass music, burley as in tobacco, bullion as in Fort Knox, and bloodstock as in horse racing." He snapped off a one-second grin. "Can I interest you in more magnificent artwork?"

"No. I want you to tell me about the fake Hopper." She looked deadly, serious.

"Ah. You know more about it than you're letting on."

"Tell me what you know." Her mood brightened.

"Well, I happened to be at the Farnsworth Museum many years ago, photographing watercolors that I had an interest in copying, or forging as you call it." He gazed at her ominously. "When I was getting into my car, who do you think I saw carrying a crate away from the museum?"

She grimaced and blurted, "I took it to pay for college. I have regretted that my whole life. A lot of good it did me. When I tried to sell it, they told me it might be a forgery." Tina turned her back and looked out the window.

"Yeah, well, I did a bad thing. I followed you back to your apartment with the intention of calling on you later to buy or make copies of the painting. When I came around, you weren't there. I asked a neighbor if she knew where you were. She said you had gone home for a couple of weeks."

"What did you do then?"

"I broke into your place, stole the Hopper, made two forgeries of it, put one back in your apartment, and hid the genuine article in the safe I have behind that wall." He jerked a thumb in the direction of the back of the shop and waited for her reaction. He feared she might try to claw his eyes out.

"Well, that explains it. I want the original back. Go get it," she demanded.

He tilted his head upward, pursed his lips, and tugged on his left ear. "Funny thing happened. About two years after I took the piece from you, it vanished from my safe. I don't know how. Nobody has the combination. Nothing else was missing."

"I don't believe you."

"To make things worse, Tina, if you hadn't brought this up, I was going to ask you to marry me."

"What? Don't be ridiculous. I hardly know you."

"There's more. I took a bunch of pictures of you walking away from the freight door at the Farnsworth carrying the painting. They're in the safe back there."

She blustered, "A wedding present for me, is that it?" Tina ruminated and paced before padding toward the front door. She looked up at Miles and said, "I am strangely attracted to you, and we've both done some bad things. I can't believe I'm saying this, but you still have a chance with me." She marched out in high dudgeon.

The Haunted House looked small and garish hanging on the sage-colored wall of the indoor esplanade at the Farnsworth Museum. Herringbone parquetry and cherry wainscoting seemed far too grand for a gloomy little work of art that would be passed over by visitors searching for bright yellows, greens, and reds on big canvases in gilded frames. Nonetheless, *The Haunted House* held its ground and mesmerized those who stopped and looked at it for more than ten seconds. After that, it would haunt them for days and weeks to come.

Tina and Miles sat at a white-cloth table in La Dolce Vita, not far from the Farnsworth. Behind them was a black-and-white mural of Italy. Across the room were windows that lit up the heavy beam work added to the décor for effect. The waiter brought glasses of wine. "Well, Tina, we're here at the scene of the crime to exorcise our demons. Are you ready?"

"Not so fast. I want to try and stump you one more time. Name the top five American hard-boiled detective writers of the twentieth century."

He sniffed and rattled off, "Dashiell Hammett, Rex Stout, Raymond Chandler, Ross Macdonald, and John D. MacDonald. Ross Macdonald wrote like Hopper painted."

"What I like most about you is your brains. Before we go over to the museum, I have something to confess." She froze for a second, and then said, "I can tell you how the Hopper got out of your safe and back on the wall at the Farnsworth." She glanced at him quickly and looked away.

"How?"

"Magic. After all, the piece *is* haunted."

"Right." He wanted most to know if she would marry him.

"Actually, I stole it back."

"What?"

"My neighbor said that you asked about me, and she was smart enough to get your license plate number. When I went into my apartment, I noticed that the painting wasn't exactly where I left it, so I got suspicious. I found out where you were in Boston and hired someone to figure out the combination to your safe."

"Wow!"

An odd response, she thought. "I felt guilty about stealing the darn thing in the first place, so I paid another person to sneak it back into the basement of the museum. It took them six months to find it."

"Well, at least I know what happened." He appeared nonplussed.

"That's not all," she added. "After you left to fly out here, I broke into your shop and got the negatives and pictures of me out of your safe, and took an interesting ledger about your forgery business. I'm guessing you've amassed some serious cash by now." She watched his face.

Miles suddenly looked quite proud of himself. "What say I give you five hundred thousand for each of the two Hoppers and you throw in the ledger for free? You can marry me then."

"Give me the million dollars, and I'll think about it," was her laconic response.

"Not exactly that way. I'll put the money in escrow with an agreement that you get it when you show our valid marriage license. You give me the ledger and Hoppers, and we'll get married."

She saw the flaw in that plan. "So I give you the ledger and counterfeits, and you refuse to marry me. No dice. We get married first, you set up the escrow, and then we make the swap."

He exhaled a sigh of relief. "Have I ever told you how incredibly beautiful you are?"

"No, but I already know it," she uttered, breaking her reverie.

They stood and looked at the ethereal watercolor together. Tina envisioned herself inside the front door, and Miles pictured himself looking out the attic window. She kissed him on the cheek and whispered, "Let's get out of here. We've got a lot of living to do and not much time to do it in. Come on, Kentucky is waiting for us." Tina's heels clomped unceremoniously as she sashayed toward the exit.

Once they got outside, Miles jumped ahead of her and said, "By the way, have you ever wondered why I made two copies? You know, I've made a lot of money fooling authenticators. Are you sure the one in there is the real Hopper?" He smiled like a Cheshire cat.

Swift's Inimitable Artisan Bourbon

At high noon on the Ides of March in 1792, Bridges' pistol smoked as he bent down to cut the silver monogrammed buttons from Colonel James Harrod's shirt and jacket. Next to the body were Lilliputian silver ingots and Jonathan Swift's journal. A hoary oak barrel entangled by rattan supplejack levitated oddly in a nearby myrtle thicket. Bridges returned to camp, informing Stoner, "Indians have killed the colonel. Let's vamoose."

On a foggy September morning in 1954, a man masquerading as Buster Gyre strode confidently from the main entrance of the federal prison in Philadelphia. He wore all black and had just finished serving eighteen months for refusing to testify at the theft trial of Secret Service agent Gaston Jefferson. Three pieces of onionskin paper were nestled deep in Buster's breast pocket. His glistening black hair had been marcelled with pomade. He reached the bustling road in front of the prison, where a taxi waited at the curb.

"Where you headed?" inquired the driver.

Buster heard the door creak when he opened it, then hastily replied, "One hundred thirty South Eighth Street."

Gyre entered the disordered jewelry store to find a roly-poly attendant with a comb-over that had long ago given in to alopecia. Perched on the vitrine between the two men was a cinched lockram pouch that read "John Wanamaker Furniture." Gyre scooped it up in his left hand and pivoted to face the shop's exit.

"There's no place you can hide those," the shopkeeper muttered insouciantly.

Buster turned back and patted his breast pocket with his right hand before quipping, "I know a place." He switched course again, quickly disappearing into the colloidal miasma visible through the etched front window.

Sixty-two years later, on a Thursday afternoon in July, a vermillion Harley slid into a narrow parking space at *Lost Dutchman Rare Coins*, east of Indianapolis. A lean, muscular man of thirty-five reached back to remove something from his saddlebag. He debouched, leaned into the wind, and squinted his eyes to fight off sprinkles of rain.

Once inside, he sat a russet accordion folder on the counter and proceeded to dry his European-style eyeglasses with a black hanky matching his ensemble. "Charlie Gyre. And you are?" He was redolent of cigarettes and the outdoors.

"Evan. How can I help you?" Wearing faded jeans and a carmine chambray shirt, the big man peremptorily approached the package, holstered sidearm in plain sight.

Seemingly unready to divulge its contents, Charlie eased the folder back, cocked his head to the right, and pointed at the large framed picture of a 1927 Saint-Gaudens double-eagle twenty-dollar gold coin hanging on the shop's back wall. "I know where the lost thirty-threes are," he allowed.

Evan chortled, and then shouted, "There's only King Farouk's, and it sold for seven-point-six million!"

"There's still nine missing. I can tell you where to find them. Nearly half a million Saint-Gaudens double eagles were minted in nineteen thirty-three. Roosevelt made it illegal to own gold coins unless they had numismatic value. Almost all of the thirty-threes were melted down in nineteen thirty-seven."

Charlie went on, "George McCann, a cashier at the Philadelphia Mint, slipped twenty early-date gold coins in the batch to be destroyed and took out twenty of the thirty-threes. McCann's fence was a downtown jeweler, Israel Switt. There's Farouk's coin, the ten found in Switt's lockbox, and the other nine. The Secret Service got them back, but they were stolen again."

"If you can get your hands on one, I'd love to see it." Evan sat at his computer, sensing there wasn't anything for him to see. He added, "There are actually twenty-two of them then. Two were saved for the Smithsonian. How can I find those other nine again?"

Charlie flipped open the folder and took out three pages of typewritten onionskin paper. Many of the phrases had been circled, underlined, and numbered. "Here's where. My grandfather gave me this before he died."

Evan stood to clutch the sheets. Ostensibly, they were directions to Jonathan Swift's lost silver mine. "What's the price?" Evan asked. "Matt, you want to look at this?"

On the first trip we came, Mundy got lost. We put our horses on a river called Red, in a place that was surrounded by cliffs. We crossed the river to the other side and wandered all day, and then came back to where we started. The next day Mundy said we would go down the river to the Indian Trace Trail. We went down the river two or three miles west and found it.

We wandered all that day and late in the evening on the next day, Mundy hollered out "here is the myrtle thicket" and that he knew the way from there. We went down a flight of Indian Stair Steps at the top of the cliff and crossed to the other side. We climbed up and went around west 200 yards on the second ledge and found the opening of the mine. Where the mine is, the watercourse is on a divide.

To go from the furnace to the mine, go up over the furnace and take a southeast course until you come to a remarkable hanging rock very high up with a gap between it and a high point. On the east side of the hanging rock, within about 100 yards, you will find the line of rocks the mine is in. Search diligently for the correct line of rocks. There are three lines of ledges or rocks, two above and one below. Swift said before he left the mine, they covered it with locust poles, dirt, and rocks, carefully concealing the opening to the mine.

Not far from the mine west, you will find a creek that sinks underground. On the slope across the top of the hill west, there is a big rock that looks like a buffalo sitting down resting on the slope. We cut our names on it—Swift, Mundy, Gyre, and Jefferson. You can stand on top of the hill above buffalo rock facing west and see through a hole in the top of the cliff and see the sky beyond. Not far from the drying ground west, we cut turkey tracks in under the cliff, pointing back to the mine.

Matt joined Evan from the back of the shop. There was a brief moment of silence between them that turned into perplexity and then disinterest. Charlie said, "A thousand dollars."

Matt was a big man, too. He wore an ultramarine golf shirt, gunmetal cargo shorts, and black-and-white striped Adidas flip-flops. Unless snow was on the ground, Matt's sartorial splendor was limited to that sort of outfit. He headed back toward his desk and replied obsequiously, "Sorry, this is not our sort of thing. Good luck selling it, though."

"I do have something else that might interest you, something my grandfather found when he hid those nine Saints in that lost mine." Out came a piece of desiccated paper, dated February 9, 1760, with chirography on both sides. "It's an old Kentucky bourbon recipe."

"How much you want for that?" Matt queried, who dabbled in German helmets, marbles, other eclectic collectibles, and had recently bought ten thousand wooden nickels.

"Two hundred dollars. This is the only duplicate my grandfather made from the original that literally fell apart in his hands."

"Since it's not authentic, I'll give you a hundred."

"I'll take it." Charlie's mouth puckered as he exhaled through his nose. Matt extracted a single bill from the till and handed it to him. Gyre buttoned the accordion folder, hustled out, and dried the Harley seat with his handkerchief. The rain and wind had stopped. He stowed the folder, lit a cigarette, straddled the bike, and left a streak of rubber spoor as he sped away.

Sam, another Lost Dutchman employee, handled the shop's internet transactions. He had an aquiline nose, impish monk's face, and evasive brown eyes. His dull black hair thrust forward sans tonsure. He scolded Matt, "Got taken for a hundred dollars this time. You know it's fake. There was never any lost silver mine or Jonathan Swift, other than the guy who wrote about Lilliput and Brobdingnag. I think I have your wooden nickels sold to a man in Michigan."

Matt pondered the verisimilitude of the bourbon formula and sophistry of its provenance. Piously, he retorted, "Maybe. We'll see."

Jonathan Swift, plucky Manxman of the eponymous lost silver mine, met George Mundy in Virginia in the fall of 1759. Mundy was a French boy who had once been captured and held by Indians. He had escaped, and after taking a liking to Swift, told him where a silver mine could be found in Kentucky. The following spring, Swift, Mundy, and two other men, Christopher Gyre and Shadrach Jefferson, headed through the Cumberland Gap to find silver.

Swift took along white-oak casks, a copper still, grain sacks, coining molds, and a mule train of mining equipment. When the silver mine was found the first time on June 21 of 1760, the men made whiskey and silver crowns until cold weather ran them back to Virginia. They took the same trip six more times over the next nine years, amassing thousands of silver coins.

Swift sailed to England with his fortune in late 1769. When he landed, King George III seized the silver coins and threw him in prison. Stricken blind, he never made it back to Kentucky. His secret whiskey recipe was foredoomed in the mineshaft.

Ed, ex-military and closing in on seventy years old, worked the counter at Lost Dutchman Rare Coins on Fridays and Saturdays to handle the increased walk-in trade prevalent at the end of the week. Covering his face and 50 percent of his bullet head, the one-quarter-inch-long hair above his shoulders was steel gray. He was leaning forward, elbows planted on antimacassars, when Matt padded to his desk and said, "Call your distiller buddy and have him make a batch." He handed over a copy of Swift's whiskey formula.

Ed put on cheaters, scanned both sides of the paper, looked up, and mumbled, "Cherry." In his sonorous voice of a carnival barker, Ed added, "I might want to drink that 'shine first." He let out a stentorian cackle that ended in his signature friendly stare and stilted grin.

Matt moved to Sam's corner desk, telling him, "Get on the internet and locate a burned-out white-oak barrel and find out where we can buy some blank liquor bottles."

On a slow Friday weeks later, Ed unloaded pails of liquid onto the parking lot behind the coin shop. "My pal said he pulled this stuff with a similar recipe from some of his old aging barrels. He put it in bottles to make it legal and told me to dump them to do the secret part, which I did." Ed's mammoth eyes reminded Evan of spotted bird eggs, his eyebrows of shallow nests.

Draining diluted scotch-whiskey placed in the barrel to swell the croze and stave joints, Matt chirped, "Good, good." After the trickle of liquid quit, he told Evan, "Hold the funnel while I ladle this in." Evan steadied the feeder as Matt used a measuring cup to monotonously fill the barrel with whiskey from the pails. Once full, Matt hammered in the bung and pronounced, "There, now take this thing out to the barn and let it get happy. Turn it every few weeks."

Sam asked later, "What are we gonna call it?"

"Thirty-Three Saint," Evan suggested. "You know, apostrophe thirty-three. That'll put it at the top of any list because an apostrophe comes before the alphabet."

Ed chimed in, "Nice. Let's use the tagline Jonathan Swift's Miner Bourbon Whiskey, and put a big picture of the double eagle on the front."

Matt followed with, "We'll do twenty-two bottles, one each for the rarest of gold coins."

A year later, Matt carried two whiskey cases into the shop. "Here we go, men."

"What's that?" John asked, his voice lugubrious and forlorn. He owned Lost Dutchman and worried incessantly. "What'd you buy now, Matt?" John's burnished look was built on a chestnut crew cut, tortoise-shell glasses, and natural suntan. He moved efficiently and with purpose, contrasting his temperament.

Matt replied, "This is what we paid a hundred dollars for a while back, plus what it cost us to produce these bottles." The diminution in his words wasn't reassuring. He lifted one of the bottles from a case box—black on gold, impressed wax seal, elixir the hue of carnelian. The centerpiece of the Brobdingnagian cigar-band label, Lady Liberty, coruscated. Matt posited, "Now we have to taste it."

"How will we know if it's any good?" John asked.

"By how it tastes," Evan replied peevishly.

"No," John complained. "What do we compare it to?"

Sam stood and mused aloud, "The best whiskey out there."

Leaning back in his chair, Ed wove his hands across his stomach and said, "Which is some rare old Kentucky bourbon, I think."

"Well, go get some then," John clamored.

"You can't. It's been sold out for years now, except in bars and restaurants that buy it at auction," Evan reported.

John was crestfallen but had an idea. "Ed, get your fanny over to a restaurant that has it. Order five shots of that stuff, pour them in this, and bring them back here." He tossed a small plastic container at Ed, who fumbled before grasping it cleanly.

Ed whined, "That juice is eighty dollars a throw. It'd take a couple of double-eagle gold coins to buy the whole bottle."

"I don't care, just get it," John rebuked.

Parnell Jefferson was the grandson of Gaston Jefferson, the Secret Service agent involved in the second theft of the 1933 Saint-Gaudens gold coins. Parnell had a leonine head and rubicund complexion. His ochre hair was short, coarse, and went in all directions. He wore splattered khakis and abraded work boots that stereotyped him as a bulldozer operator. Some years before, Gaston told Parnell that Buster Gyre had double-crossed him and run off with his share of the nine coins that were now worth seventy-two million dollars on the black market.

Gyre had claimed he hadn't gotten the coins from Israel Switt. Gaston shadowed Buster, trying to determine what he had done with them. The only thing that seemed mysterious was a visit Gyre had made to Red River Gorge in Kentucky. When Parnell Jefferson got a call from a coin dealer in Nebraska who had purchased directions to Swift's silver mine, purportedly in Red River Gorge, he bought the journal excerpts for $2,000.

Lost Dutchman Rare Coins closed at three that Saturday. Fifteen minutes later, five pairs of small cups of tawny liquor were lined up on the counter. Evan reflected, "You know, nineteen thirty-three was the year that prohibition was repealed, but hey, what's in a name?"

By four o'clock, as Herman Melville once wrote in *Moby Dick*, there were five "arrantest topers capering obstreperously" at the coin shop. Against the best of brands, '33 Saint had won the blind taste test.

Matt beamed, held up Jonathan Swift's 1760 bourbon formula, and crowed, "Now, we're talking. What'd I tell you, Sam? Authentic or not, this is great stuff." Matt lolled his head, bugged out his eyes, and stabbed at the rustic paper in his hand.

Sam came back, "Let's get the licenses to age, bottle, and sell this nectar in a tasting room. Cheers to Jonathan Swift and his Kentucky bourbon!"

Parnell Jefferson had been searching for Swift's mine for weeks. He had come up empty until the glorious azure Ides of October when he found the names of Swift, Mundy, Gyre, and Jefferson carved in the rock that looked like a sitting buffalo. On the nearest cliff to the east, he poked at a sketchy formation in the sandstone wall, and when some of the patchwork gave way, his hopes soared. He broke a sweat using a locust pole to clear the cave opening.

Jefferson stood outside the mine entrance with great anticipation. He knew he was on the verge of finding the nine 1933 Saint-Gaudens taken from his grandfather.

Crawling into the cave, he played a beam of light around the perimeter of the burrowed cavity. The air turned cool and damp. The soughing through the trees outside could no longer be heard. The titian sandstone surfaces in the cave were full of fluted crevices. There was no silver to be found, but behind a splintered rock on the floor, there it was—a metal cylinder.

Breathing heavily, Jefferson scrambled from the mine clutching the container. The warm air made him sweat again. He licked his lips, unscrewed the top of the cylinder, and violently jiggled out its contents. Nine coins fell into his hand. They were wooden nickels that read: GOOD FOR ONE BOTTLE OF '33 SAINT. CALL 317-545-7650.

Parnell Jefferson threw the nickels straight into the air and bellowed at the top of his lungs. John, Matt, Evan, Ed, and Sam were at that time heading west on Interstate 74 in Ed's vintage golden Cadillac.

Two Perfect Days
in Kentucky

If you ask me where to go to experience an Italian original, say tenebrism, I'll send you to Rome to see *The Calling of Saint Matthew* by Caravaggio, circa 1600. If it's quintessential Americana you're after, I'll point you in the direction of Kentucky for perfect weather, breathtaking scenery, outdoor sport, and *the* original indigenous spirit.

Arrange to arrive in Lexington on a Thursday in April or October. Hope for the backside of a high-pressure cell with an expected daytime temperature of seventy-two degrees. Book a three-night stay on the Executive Level of the Hilton Lexington Downtown, which is catty-corner from Rupp Arena, the heart of the city . . . the heart of the Bluegrass . . . and some say the center of the universe.

On Friday morning, dress in casual clothes, grab the car keys, a Sinatra CD, and load up on Starbucks java by eight thirty. Today the search begins for that elusive best Kentucky straight bourbon whiskey.

Pull out of the parking garage onto Main Street, turn left on Broadway, and go two blocks up the hill before turning to the right in front of Rupp Arena. Take this road west toward Versailles. After passing under New Circle Road, you'll be on a tongue of the Cincinnati Arch geological formation known as the Lexington Dome. The Cincinnati Arch is a structural uplift in the earth's crust that brought an ancient layer of bedrock limestone to the surface. Limestone makes for strong bones in animals (horses) and iron-free water (bourbon). Central Kentucky would be another common alluvial plain without the buckling of those tectonic plates. Antediluvian limestone is just under the surface of the massive and majestic Calumet Farm on the right. Did I mention there is thoroughbred horse racing in these parts? But of course, you knew that. A little further along is Keeneland, the finest place in the world to see a horse race.

After a few miles, turn right on US 60. Gleefully bisect the two rows of bucolic farms as you leave the outskirts of Versailles. Kentucky draws your eye on a map because it touches seven other states, like the center of a target, with the bull's eye right along this stretch of highway. Look for the brown "Woodford Reserve" sign and Grassy Springs Road (3360) on the left. Catch the wind rustling through the trees, crisp air, and green fields peppered with chestnut colts. As you pull in and park, know that Woodford Reserve is not a typical distillery, even though it looks like what you thought one would look like. Corporations are behind whiskey-making because of the obscene profits, and Woodford Reserve (aka Labrot & Graham) is owned by Brown-Forman of Jack Daniel's fame. Brown-Forman has a narrow product line and the widest marketing machine in the spirits world. Case in point: Jack Daniel's loses a lot of blind taste tests, yet sells a bazillion cases a year.

Of the dozen or so major bourbon stills pumping out "white dog," this is the only pot still in the bunch. All the rest are column stills with ten times the production capacity. The Brown-Forman marketing juggernaut quickly created too much demand for their super-premium brand. The trick then (planned from the beginning) is a tincture from the pot still and the rest from the "honey" barrels of the Old Forester inventory in Louisville. What puzzles me is why the mash in the pot still is boiled up to 160 proof (80 percent alcohol) before being watered down and put in the barrel. That's almost grain-neutral spirit (vodka) levels. Whatever, the formula is working really well. Woodford Reserve ($33) is the first candidate for best bourbon. All brands chosen today will be purchased back in Lexington for blind taste testing at the Hilton.

What you taste is affected by what you see, feel, and know. Not necessarily so in a blind taste test. Ostensibly, the design of the bottle is important—looks good, tastes good. Another layer back is the personal aspect. Jack Daniel, of course, was iconic. One can actually envision the foppish dandy imbibing. Woodford Reserve falls short on that front. Chris Morris, the bookish master distiller, is exceptionally skilled, but bears no resemblance to a moonshiner.

Study the display on bourbon-making before watching the brief promotional film. Don't take the ten o'clock tour. There will be a more informative one at another distillery later in the day. Survey the operation from the porch and decline the offer to sample the product. Tasting is *totally* forbidden in conjunction with driving a car.

Roll back out to US 60 and drive north (signs are confusing) into downtown Frankfort. Go straight on Main Street until it terminates at Wilkinson Boulevard. Turn right. Buffalo Trace Distillery, named for the buffalo path across the Kentucky River, will appear a couple of miles up on the left. Enter the grounds before the massive complex of stone and clinker-block barrelhouses. The salmon-colored, tin-clad buildings are trimmed in hunter green. This place is a real distillery.

The parking lot is situated so that to get to the gift shop, you have to walk by the corner of an imposing rack house full of bourbon barrels. The sweet smell of aging elixir wafting through the open windows will rock you back. Glance down to the right at Warehouse H where Blanton's is aging. Keep looking around, and you'll notice a black film on everything, a mold that lives off whiskey fumes.

The best bourbon is not a one-off. There surely has been that one barrel over the last 225 years that held the finest tasting spirit ever made. It could also be said that Sinatra once gave a live concert where he sang better than his recordings. We'll choose from widely available bourbons, not one that is a boutique, limited-edition bottling.

Sixty years ago, the now-closed Stitzel-Weller Distillery made Old Fitzgerald and W. L. Weller— the wheat-based bourbons once deigned the best. They were affordable, plentiful, and had the plucky raconteur Pappy Van Winkle behind them. Why did the distillery close? Because times changed, other great bourbons emerged, and the demand for super-premium brands began to follow the trends of the scotch business.

Buffalo Trace now produces the delicious Van Winkle formulas that are aged longer. Older bourbons are temperamental. When they're good, they're really good—when they're bad, they're horrid. Buffalo Trace has also claimed the rest of the high-age market with intermittent releases of titles (George T. Stagg, Eagle Rare) that aficionados proclaim to be of "desert island" quality.

The game changed when Blanton's came on the scene at this distillery in 1984. Maker's Mark had delivered the knockout punch to Old Fitzgerald and W. L. Weller, and then somebody got the bright idea to skim off the best-tasting barrels in the warehouses. Why throw them in with the average stuff? Why not put them out as "single barrel" or "small batch"?

It's wise to stay away from "single barrel" products because they're too expensive and by definition, don't have a consistent taste profile. "Small Batch" expressions are repeatable, available, and affordable. Therefore, if we can't use Blanton's or the eponymous Elmer T. Lee as the second candidate for best bourbon, let's reach back to a legacy Pappy Van Winkle brand, W. L. Weller Special Reserve ($19). Buffalo Trace picked up the title and formula for it somewhere along the way. It was the first wheat-based bourbon ever made.

Go back toward downtown Frankfort on Wilkinson Boulevard and turn right on Highway 127. Gaze both ways at the Kentucky River cataract and limestone Palisades. Continue straight on the 127 Bypass. After Lawrenceburg, just short of the Bluegrass Parkway, Bonds Mill Road (513W) on the right will lead up to the Four Roses Distillery. Their skimmed-off versions come in both "single barrel" and "small batch." This distillery looks like a Spanish mission, is owned by Kirin Brewery of Japan, hauls its "white dog" across the state in tanker trucks for barreling and aging, and the still itself sits across the road from warehouses owned by Wild Turkey. That said, Four Roses Small Batch ($27) deserves a spot at the blind taste-test table.

Back on 127, turn right and then right again to head west on the Bluegrass Parkway. Go south on Highway 555 to Springfield and then take Highway 55 and stay straight on Spalding Road into downtown Lebanon. Stop at Joe's Deli on Main. Pick up a couple of wraps, sides, and drinks for a picnic-table lunch at the next distillery. Proceed west on Main Street and catch Highway 52 west to Star Hill Farm near the town of Loretto.

Maker's Mark is an unabashed tourist trap, a testimony to Bill Samuels, Jr. (son of the founder) and his marketing genius. The man is likable, self-deprecating, smarter than he lets on, and a straight talker. His wheat-based bourbon is whiskey on steroids. Bill Samuels, Sr. started up in 1953, shipped the first cases to Keeneland in 1959, and from then until the company landed on the front page of the *Wall Street Journal* in 1980, he and Bill, Jr. systematically "tore down the smokehouse" of the Van Winkles over at Stitzel-Weller.

Picnic tables are next to the Samuels family home, the Distiller's House. Enjoy a leisurely lunch. This place outclasses other whiskey operations because it has an antebellum, real Kentucky feel. Take the one thirty tour and learn how great bourbon is actually made.

The buildings are blackish-brown with fire-engine-red, bottle-cutout shutters. The first thing inside the stillhouse is the copper tail box with the "white dog" flowing through it. The floor vibrates from the chugging of the two massive column stills boiling mash. This operation is a "going Jesse." The fourth corporate owner, Suntory of Japan, is keenly aware of that. The place mints money!

The brain trusts at Maker's and Woodford understand that high-volume, premium-priced brands are the most profitable. There is, however, the lesson learned from the Van Winkles, which is not to get caught in the declining phase of a product life cycle. Bill Samuels, Jr. certainly had a good reason to put out another title after fifty years. It was also a good excuse to make improved bourbon, one that would be his creation.

Maker's 46 hit the shelves in 2010. It's better than the product of fifty years. I don't buy the "just different" theory. The bourbon heavyweights are all vying for the same piece of the premium market. In Maker's case, they're barreling the product twice with special loose wood thrown in during the second barreling. Jim Beam tried the rebarreling trick several years ago with a whiskey called Jacob's Well. Beam had so many bourbon titles that there was no way the brand could get its snout in the marketing trough.

There is a twist. Maker's master distiller, Kevin Smith, had a hand in Maker's 46. It's fortuitous that he started his career working at Stitzel-Weller, the same place the senior Samuels once worked. He knows exactly how Old Fitzgerald and W. L. Weller were made. He moved to Jim Beam, and then over to Maker's, and now his still at Maker's is part of the Beam group. This sets up an interesting battle of sorts. Maker's 46 ($41) is the fourth candidate for best bourbon. We'll see how it stacks up against Weller now made over at Buffalo Trace.

The recipes are similar for both brands. Each uses 16 percent wheat, but 46 has 70 percent corn and 14 percent barley while Weller has 76 percent corn and 8 percent barley. Both follow a similar distilling and barreling pattern. Each distillery claims to do it better than the other. The major differences come at the end of the process. Forty-Six is five or six years old and uses that "voodoo" wood. Weller stays in the barrel for seven years. Can Pappy possibly get revenge from the grave?

There is one other major difference: price. The Goldring family out of New Orleans (owner of Buffalo Trace) doesn't spend the marketing dollars that Suntory (owner of Beam, Maker's) does, hence the pricing power of Maker's 46 and other high-profile "small batch" brands. In fact, Weller will be the best-priced bourbon in the tasting group. Begs the question, does value have anything to do with picking a winner?

Upon exiting, go right on Highway 52 through Loretto and take Highway 49 to the right, Highway 152 back to Springfield, and then retrace 555 back to Bluegrass Parkway. Shoot back to US 127 and go north into downtown Lawrenceburg. Take a right (east) on Highway 62. Turn right on Highway 1510 and pull into the Wild Turkey gift shop. The conspicuous compound of buildings is perched on a hill overlooking a bend in the Kentucky River.

Don't waste time going over to the distillery. The place, now owned by Campari, is drab and industrial. Jimmy Russell never really cared much how it looked. He made bourbon there for over sixty years. His son Eddie Russell is now the master distiller. They're country gentlemen, the kind of people that are all "go" and no "show." Wild Turkey is over distributed. Most people drank too much of it in college, and don't have fond memories of its finer points. Here, though, is bourbon unlike any other. It comes off the still at a lower proof, is put in a heavily charred barrel at a lower proof and goes in the bottle at a higher proof.

More "impurities" that create the flavors are left in. Rye is the flavor grain instead of wheat, similar to Four Roses and Woodford Reserve. We'll eschew the "single barrel" Kentucky Spirit and namesake Russell's Reserve for the "small batch" gem Wild Turkey Rare Breed ($38).

Get back on Highway 62 and turn right to cross over the Kentucky River. The palisades are incredible. There are now five best bourbon candidates, one each from all but one of the state's major whiskey producers. Crank up Sinatra. It's time to see the best view of the Kentucky River. Continue east on Highway 62 for six miles, turn right on Falling Springs Boulevard, and then right on KY 33. Follow along thirteen miles until the road ends at US 68. Turn left toward Wilmore, right on Highway 1268, and take a right finally on Highway 29 (Lexington Avenue). Four miles further is High Bridge, steeped in Kentucky history.

James Harrod (Harrodsburg) roamed these parts looking for a place to settle in 1774. His party and religious anomalies that came later, the Shakers, laid claims to land right on the other side of the river. Relax, slow down, take a deep breath, and reflect on God's marvelous creation. Leave behind the pressures of work and cacophonous city sounds. Feel the sun setting in the west.

Highway 29 goes back to the Hilton in Lexington. Just before New Circle Road, stop at Liquor Barn in Beaumont Centre. Buy all five bourbons (in pint bottles if available) that have been chosen, small plastic cups, crackers, and bottled water. Load everything in a small case box that will be easy to carry up to the hotel room. With the barkeep's permission, move the bourbons into the little bar area on the seventeenth floor. Set out five plastic cups. Share your plan with the bartender for conducting a quick blind taste test before going to dinner. Tell him to pour an ounce of the different bourbons in the cups. He's to make note of the brand in each but not tell you.

After returning to your room to freshen up and change clothes, step back into the bar to start the official bourbon taste test. I'll intervene here to tell you how it went for us. Sample Number one: Nose: citrus, butterscotch, oak. Taste: fudge, nutmeg, molasses. Finish: long, dry, cinnamon. Take a small bite of cracker and chase it with a sip of bottled water. Sample Number two: Nose: vanilla, cedar, clove. Taste: licorice, caramel, spice. Finish: long, cool, sweet. Sample Number three: Nose: tobacco, orange, mint. Taste: maple, raisin, cumin. Finish: warm, peach, almond. Sample Number four: Nose: apple, honey, marzipan. Taste: toffee, wheat, fig. Finish: long, sweet, buttered corn. Sample Number five: Nose: charcoal, pear, honeysuckle. Taste: cherry, rye, apricot. Finish: long, hot, violet.

We cut the group to three by pushing away numbers one and four. Two, three, and five were markedly different from each other, yet very good. Two tasted sweet, three heavy, and five floral. It would have been nice to know which two had been rejected, but I didn't ask.

Dinner is at Dudley's on Short. Exit the rear of the hotel on foot and go slightly east on Main Street. Take a quick left on Cheapside. The restaurant is straight ahead. Get a reservation well in advance of your trip. The place is busy and loud. Over crème brûlée dessert, form a bias in favor of the couple of distilleries that seem capable of making the best bourbon. Three of the five are near the north-flowing Kentucky River. The other two are essentially in the middle of nowhere. Is it the water, recipe, yeast, barrel, age, distiller?

On the way back, duck into Bluegrass Tavern to see the 200 or so different labels behind the bar, many no longer available at Liquor Barn. Heaven Hill is the only major producer of Kentucky bourbon that is not represented in the taste test. For the first alternate, their longtime-great, former Stitzel-Weller brand Very Special Old Fitzgerald ($34) or newer version Larceny ($34) are excellent wheat-grain choices. Half the bourbon titles out there are brands secretly distilled by Heaven Hill. Because the margins are so good in whiskey, intrepid marketers ("wagon peddlers") make up phony distillery names, fly under the radar, and eke out a living.

It's time to eliminate one of the three remaining candidates. Follow the same protocol as before. Can you tell with confidence which is which from the previous tasting? If not, crowning a king is going to be pretty tough. Take a second taste of each to be sure. After another confab, we pushed away the cherry, rye, apricot-tasting dram.

The two finalists stack up like this:

Number 1: Nose: vanilla, cedar, clove. Taste: licorice, caramel, spice. Finish: long, cool, sweet.

Number 2: Nose: tobacco, orange, mint. Taste: maple, raisin, cumin. Finish: warm, peach, almond.

April and October Saturdays in Lexington have a certain sense of anticipation related to horse racing. The best hundred-pound jockeys in the world pilot thousand-pound animals bred to run really fast. The aesthetic alone draws a crowd. Sneak in the human propensity to wager, and there is a patina of respectability and class to the whole thing. That comes crashing down if the slot machines arrive.

Get up late and put on a coat and tie or dress or pantsuit for an afternoon of racing at Keeneland. Hit Starbucks again by nine thirty and drive to the right on Broadway instead of left. This morning's adventure is a trip to Claiborne Farm, and magical drive through horse farm country that ends at Keeneland.

Broadway turns into Paris Pike. Seventeen miles out, in downtown Paris, turn right on East Tenth Street, and then stay right on Highway 627. The Claiborne Farm entrance (about a mile up on the left) is not very prominent. To get permission to visit, call several weeks in advance and ask politely for a ten o'clock tour. The farm allows visitors so that grooms can earn tips showing off the stallions and breeding barn. The place is spooky quiet. There are 100-year-old sycamore trees everywhere. The grounds are old but immaculate. This is the longest-running, best-known breeding farm in the world. Mr. Prospector stood at stud here for twenty years. His progeny are unequaled in the history of horse racing. Be sure to see the "teaser" for the mares. He's a pipsqueak with a floppy black mane, big teeth, and long eyelashes.

Veer over to the cemetery after a lesson on horse breeding. Famous racehorses are buried there, most notably Secretariat. He was a notch above Man o'War, John Henry, and Cigar. Secretariat still holds several track records. His offspring were duds. Be sure to tip the groom well and thank him or her profusely.

Retrace your steps about halfway back to Lexington. Turn right on Iron Works Pike (1973) and take it past the Kentucky Horse Park. Go south on Interstate 75 and then immediately west on Interstate 64 to Exit 65. Head through Midway, turn left on Old Frankfort Pike, and right on Highway 1969 (Elkchester Road), passing by the Back Gate of Keeneland. Turn left onto Versailles Road and go a short distance up the hill to the Old Clubhouse Lane entrance. After driving by a number of incredible horse farms, you'll not be surprised by the size of the crowd. Valet park, but know that it will take a half-hour to get the car back. Acquire tickets weeks in advance for a good spot in a dining room with a buffet. Races start after one p.m. and run every thirty minutes until five p.m. or so.

When the starting gate flies open, the excitement builds until the homestretch exposes the class and conditioning of each horse, and luck and skill of each jockey. The colors of the silks, flora, sibilant throng, and rolling hills in the background are there for everyone to enjoy, rich and poor, gambler and goof. The sport feels elitist, but isn't. You often catch a sharp-dressed fellow seriously discussing picks and having bourbon with a chap of lesser means. Lexington is a pristine place unspoiled by heavy industry. Central Kentucky has a natural beauty that is accentuated by nature. Even the brightly dressed women at the track somehow seem healthier and more attractive than in other places. By now, you have totally forgotten about the things in life that wear you down. Keep that feeling. Life is proverbially too short.

Besides Dudley's, there are two downtown restaurants that have been in business for a long time. One is the enigmatic Columbia Steak House on North Limestone. If Ruth Fertel had stumbled onto it instead of Chris Restaurant & Bar, the largest beef chain in the world would be Ruth's Columbia's. They've been doing salad, steak, and baked potato since 1946.

Today it's a tired place stuck in a time warp. What happened? Since the fifties, they've served a "Diego Salad" of chopped lettuce, onion, celery, tomatoes, and radishes that has a sweet oil and vinegar dressing, which is addictive. They practically invented the modern-day, hotly cooked filet with melted butter and au jus. There must have been a person like Ruth Fertel that had the passion to do it right. Passion keeps the quality of everything very high. Oddly, Columbia's has the markings of an operation that has been used as a cash cow. Big bourbon distilleries have become that way too since the corporate suits and number crunchers have won out over the onsite caretakers. It's bad enough that they are rolling out whiz-bang, one-off releases every two or three months priced at $89.99 a bottle . . . shameful, short-term thinking. I've got a hunch that Bill Samuels, Jr. and Jimmy Russell drew lines in the sand at some point to preserve the quality and integrity of their creations.

Before going to dinner, the king must be crowned. Set up the two finalists for best bourbon. Their taste should be familiar to you by now. This time, send your loved one around the corner while you pick. Have the barkeep jot down your choice. Stick the note in your pocket without looking at it. Have your mate follow the same drill. Tip the bartender nicely for playing along and helping out.

Le Deauville (reservations recommended) is the other restaurant in Lexington that has been around long enough to demand your patronage. Walk four blocks east on Main Street and two blocks to the left (north) on North Limestone. The joint looks like a tired French country bistro. The colors are garish, teal outside, buttercream walls, and a mustard, tin ceiling inside. The tables and floor are dark wood, booths bordello red. It goes to show that good food can always overcome a campy environment.

It's time for a cocktail to celebrate two perfect days in Kentucky, and discovering the best bourbon in the world! "Waiter, please bring me this one on the rocks, and that one the same way for my wife." We handed him the notes from our pockets without looking at them. Let it be a surprise.

He returned and asked, "Who gets the Maker's Mark, and who gets the Wild Turkey?"

"She gets the one that was written on the note she gave you," I replied nervously.

He shot back, "Well, I'm sorry, sir. I didn't pay attention to which was which. I have the Maker's in this hand and the Turkey in this one."

"Give me that one to try." I was disappointed in two things. We had selected different winners, and I hadn't thought ahead enough to give the waiter proper direction. The one he handed me was not the one I had selected as the best bourbon. I handed it across the table and said to the waiter, "The one in your other hand is mine."

My wife offered, "Well, these certainly *have* been two perfect days . . . Cheers!"